You're DEAD, David Borelli

You're DEAD, David Borelli

by SUSAN M. BROWN

✕

A JEAN KARL BOOK

ATHENEUM BOOKS FOR YOUNG READERS

For my mother and father, Isabel and Jack Simpson,
who taught us about loyalty and love

I would like to thank the many kids who read and commented
on *You're Dead, David Borelli* during its creation.
    Kyle McLeod and William Watson offered well thought
out suggestions, for which I am extremely grateful. I would
also like to thank the kids in Mr. Held's class at Phantom Lake
Elementary School who patiently explained to me the
fine points of soccer.

Atheneum Books for Young Readers
An imprint of Simon & Schuster Children's Publishing Division
1230 Avenue of the Americas
New York, New York 10020

The text of this book set in Dutch 809

First edition
Printed in the United States of America
Library of Congress Catalog Card Number: 95-60384

CHAPTER

1

David slid the CD into the player and adjusted the volume up—way up. As the music exploded through his bedroom, he tossed a ball of crumpled paper into the air.

The game began.

David whapped the wadball up toward the ceiling with the inside of his foot. The ball dropped back toward his bed.

"It's a high kick to the outside, but Borelli is too fast!" David yelled announcer style. He twisted. He dodged. He dived across the thick carpet and smacked the ball with the flat of his hand.

Dribbling across the bed, bounding around the desk chair, sliding behind the TV and stereo speakers, David kept the paper ball flying. He whacked it with the sole of his foot and kneed it high, then with a hard drive shot it through the lampshade goal.

The orchestra's cannons thundered.

"Yes!" David raised both fists and pranced around the

room. "David Borelli, world champion wadball player!"

Victory bells rang out. Fists still upraised, David leaped onto his bed, bouncing high. The winner again.

The door to his room swung open. The housekeeper, Mrs. Rizutto, frowned, walked over to the stereo, and switched off the triumphal march.

David lowered his arms.

Mrs. Rizutto stood with her hands on her hips. "Too much noise," she said.

Eyeing the open door, David slid off the bed. "Is Dad home?"

She shook her head. "Not yet. Maybe not till late. But you play quiet, eh?"

"*The Eighteen-Twelve Overture* isn't about quiet. It's about winning when the other guys are bigger and stronger. My mother liked this music."

Mrs. Rizutto glanced over at the framed photo of David's mother beside his bed. Marie Borelli had her arms around David and was smiling into the camera. The picture was taken before she became ill.

Mother and son were alike. Straight pale hair, long pale faces and bodies, and wide blue eyes that seemed to look through you. Too much alike, mother and son. Fragile. Mrs. Rizutto thought about her own sturdy boys. She was the lucky one.

"I'll turn off the music when my father comes home," David said.

"All right. But not so much jumping. All the way to the kitchen—boom! I hear you jump off the bed. You break your arm and then what does your father say to me?"

David smiled. "He says, 'That kid's more trouble than he's worth, eh?'"

Mrs. Rizutto tried to frown, but she laughed and gave him a hug. "I have to go home now. So you be a good boy. I've made a casserole—a good casserole—in the oven. You eat up and maybe you get big and strong like my boys. But leave some for your father. He might be hungry after his late meeting."

"Okay." David nodded. "Don't worry, I'll be fine. I'm nearly thirteen—even if I'm not big and strong like your boys."

Mrs. Rizutto eyed him to see if he was upset or maybe joking her, but his calm face told her nothing. It never did. Only the weeks of red eyes in the mornings after his mama died told her what David felt.

David watched until Mrs. Rizutto left and shut the door behind her.

Should he go eat the casserole? She'd fuss tomorrow if he didn't. His father probably wouldn't be home until very late, and he would've eaten in a restaurant or something.

Even when David's mother had been too sick to get out of bed, David's dad hardly came home. Mrs. Rizutto looked after Mrs. Borelli; David loaded up the stereo system so his mother's favorite music would keep playing while he was at school. When he was home, if she was awake, he read to her. If she slept, he played frantically silent games of wadball.

And then she died.

David took a deep breath, crumpled up another ball of paper, and turned on the CD player.

As the music began, David Borelli, world-famous wadball star, raised his fist to the sky and whammed home another goal.

David got up late the next morning. He'd stayed up to watch David Letterman and then the late movie. His father didn't come home.

The Lakethorn Academy bus was honking at the foot of the long driveway, so he had to run. As usual he headed for a seat two-thirds of the way to the back of the bus.

"Hi, Borelli," a couple of the boys called.

"H'lo, David," Elizabeth Perkins said. She was sitting beside Matt Brecken, the captain of the soccer team.

David blushed and muttered, "Hi." He slid into his seat and stared out the window. If Elizabeth ever sat beside him, he would die and go to heaven. Or if he held her hand . . . or . . .

No way. Get a grip, he told himself.

The bus picked up a few more kids, then rumbled down the tree-lined streets to the academy. With the others, David swung off the bus, shivered in the October wind, and hurried up the stone steps.

The wood-paneled halls roared with kids' noise. The little ones giggled and screeched. Down the curved stairs the older kids laughed and slammed locker doors. David headed to his own locker.

"Hey, bacteria brain, did you do your math homework?" Ted Gutenberg blocked his path. "I need the answers."

David pushed past. Ted grabbed his collar and would have twisted, except that Mr. Peiffer came out of the science lab and twisted Ted's collar instead.

"Sir!" Ted gobbled. "What's wrong? I didn't . . ."

David smiled and went to his locker. The Lakethorn Academy didn't encourage bullies. Ted would get grounds cleanup duty.

It was after the first guest on *The Late Show*, when David was eating another helping of Mrs. Rizutto's meatloaf, that the banging started at the door.

David froze. People don't knock on doors after midnight. Not unless there's something really wrong. Or unless they're robbers. His bare toes gripped the tile.

He could hear their voices.

"No one home," a harsh voice said. "Think he got wind and ran?"

"There's a light on," a softer voice pointed out.

Bam! Bam! Bam! The knocker hammered against the door.

David darted across the kitchen and switched off the lights.

"Hey, there is someone in there!"

Bam! Bam! Bammety-Bam!

"Open up! This is the police!"

David stood, glued to the floor. Panting. Sweating. What was he supposed to do?

What if they *were* the police?

What if they were lying?

Rap-Rap-Rap-Rap! They were at the window!

"Go away!" David clutched behind him for the drawer where Mrs. Rizutto kept her sharp knives. His fingers curled around a heavy handle.

Crash. Wood splintered. The alarm system screamed.

The back door flew open and slammed against the wall.

Two men—with guns—stomped into the room. One wore a police uniform. He flicked on the lights.

The big man in regular clothes swore loudly and shoved his gun back into its shoulder holster, then switched on a walkie-talkie. "There's a kid in here!"

The uniformed officer went to the control panel for the alarms and shut them off. He didn't put his gun away.

David backed against the counter, holding the knife in front of him. Ready.

The big man held out his hand in a calming gesture. "It's okay, kid. Look, we're the police." He reached into his pocket and flipped open a badge. "Go open the front door," he told the uniformed officer, then turned his attention back to David. "Is your dad home?"

David didn't move. He couldn't.

The uniformed officer came back accompanied by a small man who was obviously in charge. He glanced over at the broken door and shook his head, then turned to David. His eyes flickered over the knife.

"Ready to defend the home front, son?" His face was lined and dark but not so scary.

David lowered the knife and nodded.

"I'm Detective Arles. You're David, aren't you?"

David nodded again.

"Good. Anyone else here?"

David tried to think of what he should do or say. He couldn't think.

"Better check upstairs," Detective Arles said.

David stood still, feet freezing, breathing hard, while the big man and the uniformed officer went upstairs. He could hear their voices and footsteps as they went into each room, one by one. Then they came back.

"Nothing, sir," the big man said. "Looks as though someone packed in a hurry, though."

The detective looked at David. "Where's your dad, son?"

David looked down at the floor. How should he know? After the policemen left, he decided he'd try for twenty goals before the music ended.

CHAPTER

2

*B*ut the police didn't leave.

Detective Arles took David into the seldom-used living room and sat him in the corner of the white sofa. David heard the other officers opening and shutting drawers, and tramping all over his house.

His dad always said, "Never show them you're scared." David didn't know if it showed.

The detective settled into the opposite armchair. "We really need to find your dad," he said. "Seems he's packed a suitcase. Any idea where he's gone to?"

David shook his head. "He didn't tell me."

The detective nodded. "No problem. Who's been looking after you?"

"Mrs. Rizutto. Our housekeeper."

"We'll call her. Can't have you here by yourself all weekend, can we?" The detective sounded reassuring.

David thought that was really funny. If he weren't so scared, he would've laughed.

Even Mrs. Rizutto didn't know his dad only came home sometimes. David always used two plates and put half the meatloaf or casserole down the garbage disposal.

He thought his mom would want him to cover for his dad. She'd said if family wasn't loyal, there was no family.

The big man came into the room and gave Detective Arles an address book that had belonged to David's mother.

"We'll need to borrow this," he told David.

"Why?" David demanded. "Why are you looking for my father?"

"Don't worry about it, kid," the big man said.

Detective Arles frowned. "We think he's been using some money that doesn't belong to him. We need to ask him about it. That's all."

"Not drugs?" David pursued.

The detective looked startled. "No. You think we should worry about drugs?"

David shook his head. "It's always drugs . . . on TV. The cops make a drug bust."

The big man laughed. David felt the heat rise in his face.

Detective Arles didn't laugh. "Not always drugs. Not in this case. Just some money being moved around that shouldn't have been."

He stood up. "Well, this isn't getting us anywhere. Did you call Officer Siska?"

The big man nodded. "Yeah. She'll be here in about an hour."

Detective Arles yawned. "Okay. I'm heading home. You keep an eye on David until she gets here. Call me if Borelli shows up."

The big man snorted. "He won't."

Detective Arles left.

David must have fallen asleep in the corner of the sofa, because a woman was gently shaking his shoulder.

"David . . ."

He sat up quickly, taking a sharp breath of air.

"Hi. I'm Officer Siska. How ya doing?"

David stared at her owlishly.

"Forget it." The big man watched from across the room. "I don't think the kid's all there." He tapped his temple.

"I'm doing fine, thank you," David said loudly. Lakethorn Academy intended for all its students to be presidents of big corporations. How to speak up firmly and politely was the first lesson. David glared at the big man. "Did you find my father?"

"Not yet. But we will. Why don't you tell us where he is?"

"Because I don't know. Maybe his office." David was suddenly thinking clearly. If his father had done something wrong, he'd never go back to his office. If he was innocent, that's where he'd be sooner or later. Not here.

"Let's go pack a bag for you, David." Officer Siska gave a dirty look to the big man, then instantly smiled at the boy.

David sighed. He knew that look. It was the soft-eyed, softheaded, poor-little-boy look that Mrs. Rizutto and half the teachers gave him.

"Why do I need to pack?"

"Well, we can't leave you here by yourself. And we don't know when your dad will be back. But we'll let him know where you are."

David felt a surge of panic, but he kept his Lakethorn voice. "And where will I be?"

"We'll talk about that a little later. We have to explore some options."

"I'll stay here."

"You don't understand, David. The law doesn't allow young children to be left alone."

"I'm not young. I'll be thirteen in three weeks. Mrs. Rizutto'll look after everything."

"We called, but there was no answer," Officer Siska said. "Maybe she went somewhere for the weekend."

The other officer stood up impatiently. "Look, kid, quit screwin' around. You can't stay by yourself and you know it."

David stubbornly turned to the big man. "Mrs. Rizutto will come."

"Not for free. Your old man's been fired and there's no cash, kid. We've checked all this out. He helped himself to thousands. Creditors are ready to grab everything— including the house."

"Stop it." Officer Siska turned on the big man. "You're scaring the child."

"I'm telling him the truth." He dropped his eyes, though, and flushed a little. "Maybe this rich brat should know where all his toys've been coming from."

Siska took a step toward the other officer. "I'm warning you."

David stood up. "I'll pack. By myself."

He ran upstairs and into his father's room. Things from the tidy closet were in rows on the bed. Empty shoe boxes. Empty leather jewelry cases. Exercise weights. Unopened bottles of aftershave and cologne. College yearbooks. Old photo albums. A big suitcase.

David tore into the closet, throwing shirts and slacks and jackets onto the bedroom floor. Where was his dad's overnight bag? Where was his other suitcase?

He dragged over a chair and practically climbed up onto the shelf. The travel case was gone. So was the passport.

He thumped down from the chair and started yanking open the dresser drawers. One by one he dumped the contents onto the floor. Long before he was done, he knew the passport was gone. That the stash of emergency money was gone. But he dumped every drawer anyway.

Then he went into the room his mother had had for the last months of her illness. Careful not to disturb anything, David took out her suitcase. Not the little one she took to the hospital but the medium one she'd used when they went to New York for a week.

David hated it that other people had been in here. The police had put almost everything back. But the silver-framed photo of his mom posing with her pony when she was ten years old stood in front of his baby picture, not behind it. And her diary was upside down instead of neatly placed by the bed.

Impulsively, David took the book and photos and put them in the suitcase. Then he reached up to the shelf in her closet for all the letters and drawings he'd made for her.

"Need any help?" Officer Siska called from downstairs.

"I'm nearly done," David called back. He went into the bathroom, tore the letters and pictures into little tiny bits, and flushed them down the toilet.

Then he went back to his own room. He heard the stairs creaking. The policewoman was obviously tired of waiting for him.

David put the photograph of his mother plus a couple of CDs into his bag. What now?

"Nearly ready?" Officer Siska stood at the door.

"Just a minute." David tried to think. On Monday he'd need his school clothes. He took down two shirts, a tie, and a jacket, and pushed them into the bag. Underwear. Pajamas. His toothbrush and toothpaste.

"Okay," he said to the officer.

She started to laugh, then made her face serious. "You'll need to get dressed."

David burned red. "Okay. Right."

He didn't move until he heard her *clip clop* downstairs. Then, suddenly feeling like he was going to throw up, he stripped off his pajamas and got out jeans and a sweater.

He gazed out the window as he pulled on his socks and Nikes. The sun was coming up.

David zipped the suitcase and yanked it off the bed. His dad wasn't coming back.

CHAPTER
3

They drove to the juvenile hall in Officer Siska's police car. David scrunched down in the front seat so that no one would see him.

He could just hear Ted Gutenberg: *"Hey, sludgebutt, your old man's a . . ."* A what? A thief? A crook? Or was it all a horrible mistake?

"This will just be a short-term arrangement," Officer Siska was saying. "We'll start by calling your relatives. Who are you closest to in your family?"

With an effort, David concentrated on what she was saying. Relatives. "I don't have any."

"Any what?"

"Relatives."

Wrong answer. Officer Siska gave him the poor-idiot smile again. "Oh, I doubt that. Everyone has relatives. We all come from somewhere."

Not me, David thought. His dad's parents died when his dad was a teenager. His mom said her family was dead, too, but the way she'd said it made David wonder.

"Why don't you take me to Mrs. Rizutto?"

"That wouldn't be appropriate, David." There was a pause. "Anyway, she wasn't home."

The car wheeled into a narrow driveway and stopped in a tiny parking lot. David didn't like the look of the flat-roofed, one-story building in front of him.

David and Officer Siska went in.

A tired-looking man, about thirty, sat at the reception desk.

"Morning, Clive," Officer Siska said.

"Mmm." Clive yawned and shoved some forms across the counter. "You going to fill these in?"

Officer Siska took them. "This'll only be temporary. A day or two. David's in a jam, not in trouble."

Clive looked him over. "Okay. I'll keep an eye on him."

"Good. I'll be back, David." With a whoosh of cool air, Officer Siska was gone.

"This way, David. Let's get you a bed."

David followed him into a bright hallway lined with posters. He could hear kids' voices and the clank of dishes. Clive opened a heavy door into a dormitory with eight beds.

"This one's yours." Clive took David's suitcase and stood it beside the third bed on the right. "You okay?"

David nodded.

"All right, get some sleep. I'll check in now and then."

David dropped down on the bed, kicked off his shoes, and slid under the tight, cool sheets. He hardly heard the door click as Clive left.

The next two days were a bright blur. There were seven

other boys sharing David's dorm. Three of the boys left and three more came.

An exhausted-looking woman from CPS—Child Protective Services—told David there would be a preliminary custody hearing Monday morning.

David didn't listen. He imagined himself standing, arms uplifted, before the cheering crowds: *David Borelli, champion wadball player . . . staging a comeback . . .*

"Do you understand?"

David blinked and nodded.

"Do you want to attend the hearing?"

"No."

"You're sure now?"

David nodded. "I'm sure." Sure he didn't know what a hearing was and sure he didn't care. He just wanted to go home.

No one said anything about school, but Monday morning a woman gave him and another kid three pages of math problems to do. The other boy folded his into paper airplanes and shot them around the room. The woman didn't say anything.

After lunch a young man with a stubbly mustache showed up. He told David that his name was Scott and the court had appointed him to help look out for David.

"I'm your guardian *ad litem*." He rolled the words off his tongue. "That means I'm a court-appointed volunteer who'll help look out for your interests. We don't want you lost in the system, do we?"

David eyed the man and shook his head.

Scott explained that there would be another hearing in

thirty days to decide who his guardian would be if they didn't find his dad.

"What about Mrs. Rizutto?" David tried again.

"Who?" Scott rubbed his mustache. It gave off a sound like dry leaves.

"Our housekeeper. She's always looked after me."

The man gave him the cheerful version of the poor-idiot look and shrugged. "Maybe," he said. "Don't worry. I'll look out for you. The courts and CPS will do their best for you, too."

"It doesn't matter. My dad'll be back."

"I hope so, pal. And anyway, you don't have to go to court unless you want to."

"I don't want to."

Scott patted his shoulder and left. David hoped he wouldn't come back.

Then Officer Siska showed up.

"You were right, David." She sighed. "So far we haven't been able to track down any relatives. But"—she smiled brightly—"they've found a good foster home for you. Mrs. Kagan specializes in older children. There are three other kids there. Isn't that great?"

"What about my dad?"

For a moment Officer Siska dropped her poor-idiot look. "We haven't found him yet. But don't expect things to go back the way they were, David. Not for a while. When your dad is found, he'll be charged. Trials take a long time."

"I'd like to stay with Mrs. Rizutto . . . please."

Officer Siska shook her head. "It's not possible."

"Doesn't she want me?"

NICHOLSON LIBRARY
ANDERSON UNIVERSITY
ANDERSON, IN 46012-3495

"Yes, but she has three boys, herself, and her husband crammed into a two-bedroom apartment. The state won't authorize it for a placement. She's worried about you, but there's nothing to be done. Understand?"

It took almost no time to pack his suitcase again. Officer Siska drove toward downtown. After a few minutes, they passed a university, then a lot of fancy little shops and restaurants. To one side, huge houses reared up behind stone fences and old trees.

"That's Old Belmont," Officer Siska told him. "Those mansions have property that goes all the way down to the lake. Must be nice to be rich."

They drove on. David looked behind him, watching the line of green trees and grass disappear. The houses they passed now were mixed in with businesses. The people on the streets ambled along slowly.

By a school, a group of boys lounged against a hurricane fence. Kids about his own age jogged and walked around a track circling a field of beaten dirt.

"Lift those legs. . . . Get some energy . . . ," David could hear the teacher shout.

"That's North Central," Officer Siska said. "There's a great shop program. Do you like woodworking?"

David shook his head. His parents hired Mr. Rizutto to fix things, and the only "tools" at Lakethorn Academy were computers.

The police car turned down several back streets, finally stopping in front of a saggy old brownstone. A ramp covered the steps to the porch.

"This is it." Officer Siska looked straight ahead.

"Great," David replied. He got out of the car, took his suitcase from the backseat, and marched up to the front of the house.

Never show them you're scared.

Mrs. Kagan answered the door and ushered them in. She had blonde hair, dark at the roots, and her wide face seemed loose-skinned and smeary to David. He wrinkled his nose. The house smelled strange.

"Hello, David," she said, and held out her hand.

David shook it and murmured, "I'm pleased to meet you."

"Hmm. Manners, even. What a change that'll be. A boy with manners. I bet you've got your pleases and thank-yous down cold." Mrs. Kagan laughed loudly. Officer Siska smiled. David turned flaming red.

"You go into the living room and meet Mr. Kagan," she told him. "He's watching the soaps."

David went where she pointed. The room was long, narrow, and rather dingy. A man in a wheelchair looked up with blank eyes, then shifted his attention back to a TV in the corner.

"Hello, Mr. Kagan. I'm David Borelli." David wondered if he should offer to shake hands.

It didn't matter. Mr. Kagan ignored him. Not knowing what else to do, David sat on the edge of a sofa and watched the TV show. People shouted and cried and kissed each other. It seemed as unreal as the house.

Two commercial breaks had gone by when the front door suddenly banged open. Mr. Kagan winced.

"Hey, Ma!" a boy about fourteen, big and shaggy-haired, shouted down the hallway. "I'm home, Ma. You got the milk and cookies ready?"

The boy looked in the living room, spotted David, and winked.

Mrs. Kagan steamrollered down the hall.

"Rags! I've told you not to come shouting and banging

into my house. And I'm not your mother, thank goodness! So you darn well better call me Mrs. Kagan and show some respect."

"Aw, but, Ma!" Rags protested. "That nice Mrs. Cop that parked her car out front is gonna think we ain't just a happy little family."

Officer Siska strode in, her face stern but her eyes twinkling.

"David, this is Johnny Ragsdale, one of the Kagans' foster children. Everyone calls him Rags." She turned to the boy. "And don't you push your luck. You've just about run through your options."

He smirked and blew her a kiss, then clattered up the stairs.

Mrs. Kagan glared after him. "That boy's no good."

"Too much for you?" Officer Siska asked.

Mrs. Kagan snorted. "There ain't a kid born that's too much for me. But Rags likes to make sure."

Officer Siska smiled. "That's why I brought you David. I thought you need at least one kid who won't be trouble."

Mrs. Kagan rolled her eyes. "Appreciate that, Brenda. Be seeing you, then."

"Bye, David. Be good." And she left.

Mrs. Kagan looked him over, then nodded, apparently satisfied.

"So I'm responsible for you until the court gives you over to someone else. You obey the rules, give me the respect I'm due for taking you on, and we'll get along fine. Understood?"

"Yes."

"Good. You'll be sharing a room with Rags." She started up the stairs. "And don't let that boy get you in trouble. He's no good and'll probably end up in prison someday. But till then or till he's eighteen, he's my worry. God help me."

She clumped ahead. David took a deep breath, picked up his bag, and followed her.

"Mr. Kagan and I have our bedroom downstairs. You don't go into it even if the house is on fire. Got that?"

David nodded. She didn't look back.

"We got three rooms up here—one for you boys and one for the girls. The third is storage. You stay out of it."

She reached the landing and pointed to the door on the left. "You're in there. Dinner's at six sharp. If you're late, you don't eat. Breakfast is at seven-thirty. Same thing. If you want lunch, you make it before nine at night and take it to school. Bathroom rules are posted on the door. Got that?"

"Yes." David's voice sounded odd, even to his own ears.

Mrs. Kagan looked back sharply. "Life's hard for folks like us. There's no fresh-baked cookies and milk waiting for you here. But you'll have good food and warm clothes and a little spending money if you do your chores without whining. So don't look like someone'll eat you."

"No," David managed. "Thank you."

"Hmm. You're welcome." She opened the door to his room.

"Hey!" Rags bellowed. "Can't you knock?"

"Not in my own house. You show David where everything is."

She turned and clumped down the stairs. David slowly went into his new room. A few rock posters hung on the walls. The rest of the space was covered with black-and-white photos. Some caught the sad, wrinkled faces of street people. Several were of a little girl of seven or eight.

Rags sprawled on an unmade bed, earphones on, singing

off-key. David could hear thumping vibrations from the headset.

The other bed was strewn with clothing. David looked at it doubtfully.

"Throw 'em on the floor." Rags yanked off the earphones. The music escaped into the air. "Did our dear foster mother give you her life's-no-milk-and-cookies routine?"

David nodded and found himself returning the other boy's grin.

"She's full of it. I'll show you the way to school tomorrow. But once I've done that, we don't know each other. *Comprende?*"

"Yes." David threw the clothes on the floor. Rags put his earphones back on.

They ignored each other as David hung up his crumpled school clothes and yanked open and slammed shut the drawers of the chipped dresser near his bed. He put the CDs, diary, and his baby picture in the top drawer. For a minute, David stared at the photo of his mom hugging him, then set it on the dresser beside the one of her and her pony.

"Who's that?" Rags' earphones slid around his neck.

"My mother."

"Where is she?"

"Dead."

"Mine, too. Drug overdose a couple of years ago."

"I'm sorry." It was the kind of thing Lakethorn Academy taught you to say.

Rags' face went hard. "Ya wouldn't've been if you'd known her." He put his headphones back on and savagely twisted up the volume.

David lay back on his bed and wondered if Rags' eardrums would survive. He wondered where his father

22

was and if he remembered that he'd left a son behind.

Just then the door to their room opened slowly. Rags sat up. David expected him to yell at the intruder, but instead he switched off the radio.

The girl from the photos, thin faced and straggly haired, edged into the room.

"Hey, baby," Rags said. "How'd it go today?"

The girl said nothing, but with a darting glance at David, sidled over to Rags and sat on the bed.

Rags gave her a little poke in the side. She giggled and looked down at the floor. He grinned and poked her again. She squealed and giggled, then grabbed his hand.

"School okay?" he asked.

The girl's face drooped. Her thin fingers curled and uncurled around Rags' big hand.

Rags' face flushed. "Have those kids been bugging you again, Carrie?"

She gave a shake of her head but didn't raise her eyes.

"You want me to pound them? I'm not letting anyone pick on you. Got that? That's why you got a big brother."

Carrie looked up. "You can't. You promised Mr. McLeod."

Rags swore, then turned suddenly on David.

"What're you lookin' at?"

"Nothing."

"So don't look!"

David glared long enough to show he wasn't scared, then thumped over on his side, facing the wall. He punched his pillow. What was he doing here? How was he ever going to get home?

CHAPTER

4

David stood uncertainly in front of the closet he shared with Rags. It didn't take a genius to figure out his clothes were all wrong. Rags had jeans, T-shirts, and oversize sweatshirts from sports teams. His sneakers were expensive but nearly worn out.

"Move your butt, Borelli!" Rags banged out of the bathroom.

"I'm coming!" David called.

"I ain't waitin'!" The other boy pounded down the stairs.

David swallowed, then twisted up his foot and rubbed spit on the side of his Nikes. Even with smearing the dust around, they still looked almost new. Clean white. Maybe he could scuff them up on the way to school.

"Rags, you pig!" a girl's voice screamed out. "The bathroom's soaked!"

David jumped, then forced himself to relax. It had to be Betty Joseph, the fourth foster child. She'd still been out until after he went to bed last night. Mrs. Kagan had banged pots around all evening about it. David had retreated to his room.

Forget that. What was he going to wear?

He had jeans, but his sweater was all wrong—a gray-and-white wool knit Mrs. Rizutto'd picked from an expensive catalog. David rubbed it anxiously. It smelled awful. Four . . . no five days of daily wearing since it'd been washed.

Desperately he slid the hangers around. Nothing but his crumpled white school shirts and gray pants.

He was a dead man.

"Borelli!" Rags bellowed from downstairs.

Giving up, David pulled on the sweater, then went out into the hall. A steady stream of complaints issued from behind the bathroom door. Carrie, still in her nightgown, sat scrunched up on one side of the staircase.

"Hi," David said.

She looked the other way, hiding her face. He shrugged and kept going down the stairs.

With nerve-wracking clatters and bangs, Mrs. Kagan unloaded the dishwasher. Two boxes of cold cereal, a gallon of milk, and a stack of chipped bowls sat on the kitchen table. Rags was refilling his bowl with puffed rice.

"Sit. Eat." He grinned as bits of puffed rice spouted over the table.

Mrs. Kagan whipped around and smacked him with a dish towel she'd draped over her shoulder.

"Ow!" he yelled, and grabbed. She yanked the towel from his hand.

"You clean that up!"

"Sure thing, Ma."

"Don't start on me, Johnny Ragsdale. Mr. Kagan had one of his bad nights and I'm not in the mood."

Rags shrugged and continued eating.

"Do you want an engraved invitation?" Mrs. Kagan flared at David.

He shook his head and slid onto the bench beside Rags. When Rags made no move to pass him anything, David leaned right across him to grab a bowl and the box of cornflakes. Rags barely noticed.

"I got all your school forms on the dining-room table," Mrs. Kagan told him. "I can't leave Mr. Kagan, so you'll just have to figure it out for yourself. There's counselors at that school sitting around earning a good salary for doin' nothing. . . . I should be so lucky. . . . So they may as well fix you up."

"All right," David said. "Thank you."

"Oh . . . those manners. What a gentleman." She chortled and went back to the sink.

Face burning, David stuffed a spoonful of cereal into his mouth. No milk. He forgot the milk.

He glared at Rags. "I like it this way."

Rags grinned. "Sure."

A few minutes later David waited at the foot of the stairs with his sheaf of papers while Rags detoured to the door of the girls' room, hugged his sister, and murmured something to her. She giggled.

Betty Joseph emerged from the bathroom and clattered down the stairs. David saw that she was about fifteen, wore lots of makeup and jewelry, and had her damp hair twisted into an escaping ponytail on top. When she saw David she paused.

"Hi," he said. "I'm David Borelli."

"Do I look like I care?" She headed toward the kitchen, tossing back over her shoulder, "Another loser."

David sighed and leaned against the wall. If this was home, he couldn't wait to see what school was going to be like.

Rags walked steadily ahead. Clearly he didn't want anything to do with David.

David bit his lip angrily and half ran to keep up. By the time they'd reached the school David was out of breath.

"Hey, Rags!" A bunch of guys clustered against the hurricane fence shouted to him.

"Office is through those doors," Rags told David, then strode off toward his buddies.

David wanted to throw something at him. He was so angry at being dumped again that he could've cried.

"Oh, great," he told himself savagely as he went up the steps to the front doors. "Start bawling. Make a good impression."

Inside, it was gloomy. David held his breath. He really did want to cry. He wanted to sit in the corner and howl.

"Hey!" Someone tapped his shoulder. "No one in the school before the bell."

David twisted away and swung out.

The man stepped back. David glared, chest heaving.

It was the teacher who'd been shouting at the kids to keep running when Officer Siska had first driven David past the school. As he had then, he wore a T-shirt with a whistle dangling over his chest. His brown hair was graying, his eyes tired.

David's breathing slowed under the calm scrutiny.

"New here?" the coach asked.

David nodded.

"I saw you come up with Johnny Ragsdale. Are you staying at the Kagans'?"

David nodded again.

"Well, then. Welcome to North Central. The office is that way. I'm Mr. McLeod. I'll see you in class." He pointed down the hall and started walking away.

"Thank you, sir."

The coach swiveled. His eyes glimmered with amusement. "You're welcome, sir." He kept walking.

David went to the office.

The bells for a new period had rung three times before David's registration was completed. Most of the time they kept him waiting on a hard wooden chair outside while they telephoned for confirmations, drank coffee, and filled in forms.

Finally the counselor came out and handed him a map of the school, a handbook called *Welcome to North Central Middle School*, a locker assignment, and a class schedule.

David looked at it doubtfully.

"You have one more period before lunch—social studies with Mr. Kilmer. Past the stairs, turn left, third door. Your locker is just down the hall from there."

David found his way to the right hallway and scanned the lockers. Most of them were scratched and dented, and had graffiti written on them or painted out. When he found his own he sighed. The combination seemed to work, but the latch was bent. It wouldn't shut tightly enough to lock it.

He smiled wryly. It wouldn't make any difference—he didn't have anything worth stealing.

When David walked into the class it had already started. Mr. Kilmer glanced briefly at his admit-to-class slip, then waved him toward some empty desks at the back of the room.

Without waiting for David to settle, he started talking about the American Revolution, pacing and talking, never looking at the kids.

David went toward the back. Rags, slouching in one of the seats, stared as if he'd never seen him before. One of the boys stuck out his foot. David stumbled.

"New kid! New kid!" a hugely fat boy hooted behind his hand. The other boys joined in. The girls giggled and looked him over.

Mr. Kilmer kept on talking and pacing.

David slid into an empty chair. The boy ahead of him, big and about forty pounds overweight, turned around.

"Hey, butthead. That's my seat."

David stared back, confused. Rags and the other boys grinned.

"Get outta my seat, or I'll pound the crap outta you."

"But you're sitting in that chair!" David protested.

"They're both my seats. Now move, pig breath, or I'll wipe your face off."

David hesitated. It wasn't worth it. He got up and sat in an empty seat in the next aisle.

Another boy turned around. He was about a foot taller than David and his muscles bulged where the sleeves of his sweatshirt had been cut off.

"Hey, butthead. That's my seat."

David took a shaky breath. How could he have been so stupid? The boy ahead slammed back in his chair so that

David's desk jerked backward, whiplashing his neck.

He looked up at the teacher.

Mr. Kilmer kept talking and pacing. The chair rammed back into his desk again.

"Hey, butthead. That's my seat. . . ."

CHAPTER 5

The hazing kept up all day.

Hey, butthead! That's my seat!

At lunch, wherever David sat, one of the boys ordered him to move. After the third time David went to the boys' washroom and ate half a sandwich. The rest he stuffed into the garbage.

In math David refused to change desks. Sean, who'd started it, coughed loudly while Ryan, the boy with the cutoff sweatshirt, rammed David's desk and whacked his head from behind.

In the last period, the English teacher, Miss Kidd, slammed a wooden pointer against a desk and ordered the boys to leave David alone. She threw in a lecture and gave Sean a detention.

David felt their eyes on him. He was a dead man.

When the last bell rang he raced for the back door. Nobody stopped him.

So far so good.

He scanned the paved yard and dirt field, looking for a way out. There wasn't one. The fence, eight feet high and rusty-wired on top, ran around the entire school grounds.

Maybe he could make it through the teachers' parking lot.

David gripped his books and dodged between the cars, heading toward the front sidewalk.

"There he is!" Sean, Ryan, and three more huge guys advanced on him.

David froze. Ahead, Rags was striding along the sidewalk.

"Rags!" David ran for him, grabbing the other boy's arm. Rags pulled away and glanced over at the advancing gang. For a second his eyes narrowed and his fists clenched, but then he shook his head.

"Don't let 'em know you're scared." He walked away.

"Rags!"

The other boy kept walking.

David tried to run. Too late. Ryan grabbed him.

"Hey, butthead. We wanna talk to you."

David thrashed against Ryan. No good. Ryan shoved and David fell against Sean. Grif, Brian, and Mike laughed.

"Hey, butthead. You're in my way." Sean propelled David back to Ryan.

Ryan spun him at Mike. It became a game of volleyball. David was the ball.

He tried to twist away, but they didn't let go. When David was too dizzy to stand up, Ryan bounced him by the shoulders while they all laughed. Blood splashed from David's nose onto his sweater.

He tried to elbow Ryan. The other boy laughed.

"I'll kill you!" David shouted. He kicked out, judo style. Ryan's grip held him up. Both feet slammed into Sean's stomach.

"Oof!"

"Hey, Sean, watch out for the butthead," Grif snickered. He combed fingers through his lanky red hair. "Hey, man, I gotta go."

Brian, Grif, and Mike looked David over one more time, then walked away.

Sean slowly straightened. "And now you die."

David just stood there, held up by Ryan's grip on his shoulders. He lifted his chin. He wouldn't show he was scared.

Sean rammed his fist into David's belly. David crumpled, gagging and choking. A group of girls gathered a little way off, watching.

"Sean, leave him alone," one girl called. "You're such a jerk."

Ryan let go. David fell to the ground. Sean kicked him in the thigh.

Through half-closed eyes David watched the bullies saunter over to the knot of girls.

"The guy had it comin'," Sean declared. "We're just teachin' 'im what's what."

The boys walked off. A couple of the girls kept looking back over their shoulders. David sat up and puked.

"Oh, *gross!*" one girl said loudly.

For a long time he sat with his head in his hands. When he had himself under control David got to his feet and started walking.

They couldn't do this to him!

It was his father's fault!

Before the thought could make him crazy, David shoved it out again. He'd only think about getting back at those bullies. Somehow.

At the Kagans', David hesitated by the front door, feeling like he should knock. Nope. This dump was home.

In the living room Mr. Kagan was parked in front of a game show. From the kitchen Mrs. Kagan's voice rose and fell as she scolded Betty.

Carrie edged out and scuttled down the hall. She stopped as her wide eyes took in David's muddy, blood-smeared face and clothes. She touched his scraped hand.

"Does it hurt?" she asked.

"What do you think?"

"I think it hurts. Come on."

She took his hand and pulled him upstairs toward the bathroom. She pointed at the toilet. "You sit there."

David slumped down. Very businesslike, Carrie wet a washcloth with cool water and gave it to him.

David wiped it over his face. "Thanks."

She smiled, lighting up her thin face. Then she ran to her room and came back with a tin Band-Aid box. She looked inside first, tallying up her treasures.

"How many do you need?" Her eyes were anxious again.

David shrugged. "I'm okay."

She pointed to his scraped hand, then gave him one Band-Aid.

In spite of himself, David smiled. "Thanks."

Carrie grinned, then ran back to her room and shut the door.

David sighed, stuck the Band-Aid over the scrape, and finished cleaning himself up. The knee of one jean was ripped. That could be an improvement. Half the guys wore torn jeans. Would his sweater come clean? If not, he'd be left with nothing but white shirts.

"I'm a dead man," he said, then shivered. It might be true.

Once he'd yanked on a shirt David headed downstairs. Rags was on his way up. David pushed past as though the other boy didn't exist.

In the kitchen, Mrs. Kagan sat at the table, sipping from a mug of coffee and reading a magazine. Betty Joseph had disappeared.

"Have you got a phone book?" David demanded. "I need to make a phone call."

She didn't look up. "Well, you sure lost those good manners fast enough."

David took a deep breath. "Please. It's important."

"One call a day. No more than ten minutes. Phone book's in the drawer." She gestured vaguely.

"Thank you."

David searched through three drawers before he found the directory. With it open on the dining-room table, he thumbed through until he found the police station.

He punched the number into the kitchen wall phone, then pulled the receiver around the corner into the other room.

As the phone rang, the contestant on Mr. Kagan's show won ten thousand dollars. Would that be enough money to get his father out of trouble, to get his own life back?

"Metro Police. Please hold."

David waited. When the voice finally came back on, he asked for Officer Siska.

"Juvenile. Siska here."

"Hi." David found he couldn't say anything else.

"Hi, yourself." Pause. "Who is this?"

"David Borelli . . . I—I have a problem."

"What is it, David?"

"I got beat up. At school. I don't want to stay here. You can't make me stay here!" He couldn't hold onto his Lakethorn voice. What happened to him didn't happen to Lakethorn boys. Shouldn't happen to anyone.

"Hmm. Rough first day, I guess."

"You could say that."

"Child Protective Services will have assigned you a social worker by now, David."

"I only saw her once. I don't even remember her name. You're the one that left me here!"

Pause. "I'll come by tomorrow before school. Just this time."

"Thank you, Officer. I appreciate this."

She chuckled. "Right. Till tomorrow."

The phone clicked. David hung up and returned the phone book to the kitchen drawer.

Mrs. Kagan had assigned him the weekday chores of taking out garbage and unloading the dishwasher. Rather than going up to the room he shared with Rags or sitting with Mr. Kagan, David decided to do these jobs. Mrs. Kagan had said there'd be pocket money. Would it be enough to buy a new T-shirt?

"Mrs. Kagan," he said as he put away the last glass. "How much allowance do I get? I need a new T-shirt."

"You kids always want something. . . . Isn't enough that I feed and . . ." She looked up grumpily, then blinked in surprise. "Hmm. What happened to you? Walk into a door?"

"Some guys beat me up."

She made a clicking noise with her tongue. "Guess you need more than good manners to get by."

"I could use a new T-shirt."

Mrs. Kagan looked him up and down. "Combat gear might be more use." She flipped another page of her magazine. "Life's hard, David. There's no milk and cookies for folks like us."

David leaned on the table. His face moved closer to Mrs. Kagan's.

"But is there a new T-shirt?"

A shrewd look came into Mrs. Kagan's eye. "The yard needs raking."

"I can rake."

"And the wood floor in the front hall needs polishing. Real paste-wax polish that has to be rubbed shiny—by hand."

"I can polish."

Mrs. Kagan smiled and picked up her magazine. "I think I can spare some time and a few dollars to go shopping for a T-shirt."

David let out his breath. "When?"

"When I'm freed up from worrying about the leaves all over the lawn and that dirty old wax in the front hall."

David smiled. "Hey, lady, where can a fellow find a rake in this town?"

"Try the garage, stranger."

CHAPTER
6

"Hey, Borelli." Grif elbowed him. "Great shirt. You goin' to a funeral?"

"Your own, maybe?" Ryan jeered.

The boys laughed and crowded David against the lockers before moving on. David glared after them, then straightened his shoulders.

It was going to be okay. Even though she told David he had to stay at the Kagans', Officer Siska'd promised to fix things at school.

The boys hadn't even suited up for first-period gym when the call came over the PA system.

"David Borelli, Sean Moskovitz, Ryan Michaels, Brian Goetz, Mike Jones, and Albert Griffin—report immediately to the vice principal's office."

Mr. McLeod's gaze fixed on David, then the other students. "Okay, boys. Down to the office. You'll have to make up the time in laps after school. Check with me later."

"Oh, I'll be sure to do that, sir," Sean snickered.

Mr. McLeod didn't react at all, just went on with herding the rest of the boys into their gym clothes. David picked up his books and headed toward the door. Sean came up behind him and shoved.

"Hey, butthead, you're in my way."

David ricocheted off the doorjamb. He spun, ready to flail out at Sean, but McLeod beat him to it.

The teacher had Sean by the back of the neck.

"You know, Moskovitz, I don't think you can even imagine how tired I am of your attitude." The teacher's calm eyes were only a few inches from Sean's small ones. "Think about it."

He released the boy with a shove. Sean staggered into the hall. The other boys followed, grinning. David kept his distance.

"That scumbag," Sean snarled. He thrust his finger at David. "And you, Borelli. You're dead."

The gang sauntered down the hall. David followed at a safe distance. As the boys reached the office, Officer Siska walked out past them and gave David a thumbs-up sign. She headed briskly toward the main doors.

When the guys eyed him suspiciously, David wished she'd stayed. Sean led the way into the vice principal's office.

The desk held a small sign reading *Robert Thelps*. The vice principal looked tired and irritated with all of them, including David.

"I don't like the police showing up here with complaints about my students," he said. "And I don't like a gang beating up another boy."

"Sir, we didn't hurt him. It was just a joke." Sean shoved his hands into his pockets and leaned against the door frame.

The vice principal's expression didn't change.

He knows what they'll say, David thought. He's done this a hundred times before. . . . maybe a thousand.

"Jokes don't require a police visit." He looked at David and his mouth thinned.

He's mad at me, David realized, shocked. Because I called the cops and complained.

"Sean, you've had warnings before and you signed a behavior contract just three weeks ago. Obviously none of this has made an impression. Perhaps a week's suspension will. You other boys will each get five detentions."

"What about me?" David's voice squeaked. His face grew hot.

Mr. Thelps eyed him. "No. But I hope you won't turn out to be a troublemaker, Borelli. We don't need trouble-makers at North Central. Now all of you—get back to your classes. Except you, Sean."

They left David alone for the rest of the day, but he saw them talking together and looking his way. The other kids ignored him.

Time passed in a fog. David didn't take notes or open his books. The teachers didn't care—except Miss Kidd. She gave him an extra assignment for daydreaming.

Finally the last bell of the day rang. David went to his locker and tossed his books inside. Forget the homework. He couldn't risk being loaded down. They'd be waiting for him.

In spite of himself, his feet slowed as he neared the exit.

"David!" Mr. McLeod called him from an open door marked *Photo Lab*. "What about those laps?"

Rags stood behind Mr. McLeod, holding a camera in one hand and a sheaf of black-and-white photos in the other.

"I . . . uh . . . could I do them in the morning?" Tonight the boys would be waiting. His only chance was to run for it.

Mr. McLeod nodded. "Seven a.m. sharp. Three miles—that's twelve laps around the track."

"Sure." David headed for the door. Maybe tomorrow he'd be dead.

The boys were waiting. So was the vice principal. His lips thinned when he saw David.

"Borelli, I don't want you hanging around the school. Get going. Now."

David started down the steps. The boys' eyes were ice chips as he walked by. They started following.

"Ryan, Mike, Brian, and Albert!" Mr. Thelps snapped. "I want to talk to you!"

David couldn't believe that Thin Lips would save him. His pace quickened. He didn't look back.

Once he got off the school grounds he broke into a run. They were bigger. They had longer legs. He didn't know how long Thin Lips would hold them.

His feet slapped against the pavement. Block after block. His breath burned in his throat. Why was it so far? Pain in his legs. Pain in his side.

David slowed. They couldn't catch him now. Could they?

He stopped and looked back along the six blocks. It couldn't be! They were there. Three blocks back and running. Thin Lips hadn't kept them long enough. And there were five of them now! Sean!

Seven blocks to go . . .

David ran. Desperate. Like an animal hunted by dogs. Down one street. Back up another. Lost.

Keep your head. Make for home.

Half a block from the Kagans', they caught him.

David's breath tore through his throat. His legs shook from exhaustion. The other boys were breathing hard but not shaking or panting. He lifted his chin and clenched his fists.

The five boys circled him, all grinning—except for Sean. His face was stone cold.

He grabbed a handful of David's jacket. David jerked away. No breaks in the circle.

"Hey, butthead, now you're gonna die. Hold 'im, Grif."

"No way, man. You said it was gonna be a fight, not a massacre." He grinned and gave David a push.

Sean's face flushed. "It's a massacre." He slammed his fist into David's face.

David went down. Bolts of light zigzagged in his eyes. His face had exploded. Dimly, through the pain, he heard another voice.

"Hey, Davey boy, looks like you could use a hand." Rags reached down and yanked David to his feet. David staggered and would have fallen if Rags hadn't held him up.

"Butt out, Rags," Sean snarled. "This has nothin' to do with you."

Rags grinned and propped David up like a scarecrow. "This guy is my roommate. He takes out the garbage. If you murder him, I gotta take out the garbage. This is important."

The lightning receded from David's eyes. He blinked. He wouldn't let Rags humiliate him. He'd die first. David yanked himself away.

Sean stood his ground. "This turd's ours. He's gonna get what's comin' to him."

"But not today," Rags said. "Let's go, Davey boy."

He dragged David down the street toward the Kagans'. Two doors away David puked into the gutter.

He wiped his mouth and glared at Rags. "I don't need your help."

Rags laughed. "The hell you don't. Sean is mean and he was gonna kill you."

"Now he'll do it tomorrow."

"So? Enjoy today."

In spite of himself, David laughed. "Hail, Caesar," he grunted. "We who are about to die salute you."

"Davey boy, you need a head check."

"So why'd you stick up for me today?"

Rags shrugged. "McLeod seemed to think I should."

"What'd he say?"

"Nothin' much. He just lets you know."

Down the block Sean was still glaring in their direction. David turned away. He and Rags clattered up the wooden ramp to the Kagans' and, without knocking, went in.

"Hey, Ma," Rags shouted down the hall. "We're home! You got the milk and cookies ready?"

CHAPTER

7

Somehow David got through the rest of the week. And the next. Occasionally Rags stepped between him and the other boys, but not all the time. Not often enough.

The first weekend, David finished raking the leaves and polished Mrs. Kagan's front hall until his arms hung like logs from his shoulders. But the old wood gleamed. Mrs. Kagan bought him two T-shirts and a pair of secondhand jeans.

Child Protective Services sent over a box of his clothes from the house.

Rags lifted out the expensive sweaters, jackets, and designer jeans, and burst out laughing. "Davey boy, if Sean don't waste you to get these, he'll do it to you just for wearing them."

David crammed the box into the back of the closet.

Betty Joseph helped him get the blood and stains out of his sweater, then asked if she could borrow it. He wasn't surprised that she didn't return it.

Nights David silently played wadball—except for the

photos and his mom's diary, it was all he had left from his old life. When he crumpled the paper into a ball he could hear the roar of the imaginary crowds. The wadball shot from foot to hand, from ceiling to floor, each time intercepted by his hand, his foot, his knee, or his elbow.

David Borelli —champion of the world!!!

Rags watched but said nothing. Mostly he listened to his music or rearranged the photos on his wall. The second weekend he brought home a camera from school and spent both days outside with Carrie. Monday night he pinned a new series of photos onto the walls.

"Those are really good," David told him.

Rags grunted and flushed.

"Did Mr. McLeod teach you?"

Rags nodded. "He showed me how to use a camera and develop film. I taught myself the rest."

It was David's thirteenth birthday. If Mrs. Kagan knew, she forgot. David didn't know whether to be glad or miserable.

Mrs. Rizutto sent a card via CPS. Inside was a crisp ten-dollar bill and a letter.

I try to come and see you, David. But what do you think happens? I fall down the steps and break my ankle.

I worry that you are okay. Does your foster mother cook good meals, so you can get big and strong? My Joe lifts weights now and runs on the track. Maybe you can do this, too? If you need something, you call me and I'll send my boys.

So you have a very happy birthday.

Love from Mrs. Rizutto

David smiled and decided to buy Mrs. Rizutto a get-well card. It seemed like a thousand years since he'd seen her—since he'd thought she could rescue him.

That night he lay back against his pillows thinking about the way his life used to be. Impulsively, David took his mom's diary out of his drawer. He examined the fine leather cover and the sheen of gold leaf on the tops of the pages. He could remember coming into his mom's room sometimes and seeing her bent over the book, writing away.

She didn't even have a lock on it —she trusted him not to snoop. But now that she'd been dead for months and months, it wouldn't be snooping.

And he needed to remember her—not like a dream person but as his mom. He opened the book.

The pages were very thin, like the pages of a Bible. First David looked just at the dates. Sometimes his mom had skipped days or even weeks, so the diary covered from just after her marriage to a few weeks before she died.

David turned to the first page and settled back to read his mom's fine, small writing.

The house is perfect—almost! I want to paint the trim a rich eggplanty purple color, but Tony says it'll make us look too different from everyone else. I like looking different!

I'm going to content myself with planting a Japanese-style garden. It's okay with Tony because I showed him one in a Better Homes and Gardens layout. What a contradiction he is—wanting to be the successful man everyone admires and, at the same time, worried he won't fit in. But he's such a charmer that he makes me melt inside, so who cares!

David rolled his eyes and randomly picked a page about halfway through. He smiled when he saw his own name.

Big day in our lives. David starts grade one! He looks so little in his school uniform. I wanted to scoop him up and snuggle him like he was a little baby. But he's much too dignified, my little man. After I put him on the bus I came back and cried for an hour. Guess I'm the baby.

David put the diary down. The rest of the page was about the flower bulbs she had planted around the yard. He grinned remembering how she'd walked him around, proudly showing little heaps of moist black earth. She said she had planted a couple of hundred bulbs. It had been really boring.

He fell asleep, dreaming about his mom and the masses of bright tulips that had bloomed in their garden every spring.

But the next morning, from Mrs. Kagan's strident call to the long walk to the shabby school, his new life howled through the old memories.

Each day David drifted through classes. He let the boys settle into their chairs first; then he picked one as far away as he could get. If he couldn't find a desk away from the others, he skipped the class.

Except for Miss Kidd and Mr. McLeod, nobody seemed to care.

Each afternoon he took off from the last class and ran for home. The second week he thought the guys had lost interest.

Big mistake. They nearly ambushed him by the Mini-Mart two blocks away. If David hadn't heard Grif's braying laugh, he would've been caught.

Officer Siska didn't call to see what had happened. David wasn't surprised. The woman from CPS came and talked to him. David didn't say much. There wasn't anything she could do.

The court volunteer, Scott, showed up one day. He sat at the kitchen table and drank Mrs. Kagan's coffee while David stared at him as if he were a slug. His mustache was a little longer. Now it sounded like dead grass when he rubbed it.

"Everything's going along fine," he told David. "There's been an order of publication."

"A what?"

"A formality. They'll publish a paragraph or two in the paper for the next forty-five days asking for anyone to come forward and claim guardianship of you."

"Like who?" David asked.

Scott stirred his coffee and looked uncomfortable. "They hope your dad will, naturally. If not, there'll be a final dependency hearing and you'll become a ward of the state."

Like Rags and Carrie and Betty Joseph, David thought. And he wouldn't have anyone to look out for him except his foster mother.

Pleading homework, David left Scott chatting with Mrs. Kagan. His dad had dumped him.

He could just picture Sean's gloating face: *"You're dead, David Borelli!"*

One week slid into another. October was gone, then November. David ran home a different way each night. It wasn't so hard now. His side didn't ache, and if he was out of breath, it didn't take so long to catch it again. His legs didn't shake.

Stubbornly he kept his Lakethorn voice and good manners. He *wouldn't* become like those guys. He never thought about his father. Or if he did, he made the thoughts go away. When he could.

One night he woke up to the sound of soft crying. Rags was breathing noisily, deep in sleep. Not knowing where the sound came from, David lurched out of bed and crept into the hall.

A light shone under the bathroom floor. It was Carrie.

"Hey, Carrie?" he whispered. "It's me, David. You okay?"

The silence was like an indrawn breath.

"Carrie, open the door. I'll help you." David wondered what he'd have to help with. Was she sick? Enough to wake up Mrs. Kagan? That'd have to be really sick.

The door clicked. Carrie's tear-streaked face looked through the crack.

"What's wrong?"

She just gazed at him forlornly.

"Are you sick?"

She shook her head and pulled the door all the way open. The floor was strewn with school assignments.

"My new teacher, Miss Bradley, said I had to do all my papers." Carrie's eyes streamed tears. "I don't know how and she said my mom or somebody at home was supposed to help . . . and I don't got a mom . . . and . . . and I can't do it. . . ."

"It's okay! It's okay!" David whispered. "Can't Rags help you?"

Carries eyes dropped and she shook her head.

David sighed. "When's it supposed to be done?"

"Tomorrow."

He couldn't believe this. "Well, I was awake anyway. What's first?"

There were at least six weeks' worth of papers. Carrie's teacher had left to have a baby and the replacement teacher, Miss Bradley, had only been there a week. Carrie'd been too scared to ask for help or explain.

Miss Bradley had said that if Carrie didn't do some of her work the principal would call her parents.

"Then—they won't let me c-come to school anymore," Carrie sobbed.

"No way, Carrie," David whispered. "They can't kick you out of school for not having parents."

"But she said to have m-my mom help me . . . 'cause I c-can't do my w-work."

"Well, I'll help you so Miss Bradley won't know and everything will be fine," David soothed. He tore off another wad of tissue and handed it to Carrie. She hiccuped, sniffled, and then gradually settled down.

They sat cross-legged, leaning against the bathtub. One by one they did lists of spelling words, sheets of subtraction with borrowing, a report on spiders, and questions about pioneers. By the time they'd reached the pioneers, Carrie was leaning sleepily against David's shoulder.

"Come on," David urged. "You fill the questions in. I'll tell you what to write."

He put the pencil into Carrie's hand. She roused enough to print the words he told her. Then they were done. David steered Carrie back to bed and covered her up.

Betty Joseph continued to snore softly, mouth wide open.

David got the school papers and stacked them on Carrie's dresser, then went back to his own room. Now he couldn't sleep. The night outside lightened to pale gray.

David threw off his covers, wadded up a ball of paper, and began playing in the half-light. He whacked it around the room, up, down, across his bed, and over toward Rags.

He slammed into the bed.

"What the . . ." Rags erupted from the mound of covers. "I'm gonna kill you, Borelli," he growled sleepily.

David hardly heard. His ears filled with the roar of the crowd, the admiring shouts of the announcers:

David Borelli—the orphan who fought his way up from life as a dead man—the champion of the world . . .

CHAPTER

8

"Hey, Borelli!" Grif trotted alongside David as they rounded the track during gym. "Was that your old man on the front page? Must've been, for such a high-class crime."

What was Grif talking about? What did he know about David's father?

David faltered, his face burned. "No way! Shut up!"

Grif grinned widely. "So it was your old man!"

"I told you to shut up!" David made his legs pump steadily again.

"Don't tell me to shut up!"

David kept going.

"Hey, Mr. McLeod," Grif yelled to their teacher. "David's dad is a real track star. He just runs and runs. It was in the paper yesterday—front page!"

Rags jogged up to David and looked at him curiously. David stared straight ahead.

"Albert, if you've got that much energy for talking, you're not running hard enough," Mr. McLeod called. "Take an extra three laps."

Grif stopped. "Three!"

"Make that four. On the double."

In the changing room, David kept clear of everyone and ignored the guys nudging each other and laughing.

Later, when he went to his locker, the door wasn't latched. Inside, a newspaper clipping hung on a coat hook: MAIL FRAUD LINKED TO LOCAL BUSINESSMAN.

David took the clipping down and swallowed.

Anthony Borelli, already wanted by police for the embezzlement of a half million dollars from Citywide Management Corporation, has been linked to a multimillion-dollar mail fraud. . . .

David blinked rapidly. He wouldn't cry. Not here. Unable to stop himself, he read the rest of the article.

It said more about the theft from his dad's company and that his dad was a high-stakes gambler. David hadn't known that. Detective Arles, it went on, said the police had several leads to Anthony Borelli's whereabouts and expected to make the arrest within a few days.

Behind him, David could feel the boys' eyes on him, hear their snickers. He crumpled up the clipping and threw it into his locker.

"Let's go, boys." The science teacher came out of his room. David closed the locker door with a slam. He was out of here.

But Thin Lips was prowling the hall, keeping an eye on the exits.

"Borelli, you're late." He pointed toward the science lab and watched until David retraced his steps and went in.

David slid into an empty seat. It was weird. As if a sheet of plastic a foot thick separated him from everybody else. The kids all turned in their seats and stared. A couple of the girls tried for the first time ever to start a conversation with him. David grunted answers and kept his eyes down.

After school he couldn't wait to get out. When he started the long run home, Rags caught up and kept pace with him. Rags said nothing until the third block.

"So you wanna be a track star?"

David clenched his fists and kept running.

"North Central don't do track competitions."

David noted that his breath was still regular. No pains in his side anymore.

"Soccer. We do soccer. I'm center forward. Maybe you wanna try out for soccer?" Rags grinned enticingly.

David stopped. "I don't want to run track. I don't want to play soccer. And I don't want to see your ugly face!"

He started running again. Rags kept pace.

On the eighth block Rags began to run out of wind. David was breathing hard but was still okay.

"Mr. McLeod thinks you oughtta go out for soccer, too," Rags puffed, and slowed to a walk. David kept going. "And by the way," Rags called, "Kristi thinks I got a real cute face."

David turned around and shouted, "Then she's gone

blind and weird!" He sprinted the rest of the way to the Kagans'.

He slowed as he passed an unfamiliar blue car parked by the sidewalk—Mrs. Kagan never had visitors except social workers. That was the last thing he needed today.

David sat at the top of the wooden ramp, breathing hard. Sweat poured off him, as if he were being cleaned from the inside out.

Rags jogged up and sank down on the ramp beside him. "I mean it, Davey boy. You oughtta go out for soccer. Our team hasn't won in three years. It's great."

David snorted. "Yeah, that sounds really great."

Rags grinned. "We are at the rotting wet bottom of the compost heap. Anything makes us look good. Even you'll look good."

"What if we lose?"

"We've done it before." He got up. "Think about it."

David shook his head.

Suddenly the door swung open. Mrs. Kagan glowered at them.

"It's you!" she accused.

Rags and David looked at each other in bewilderment. David got up.

"Well, get in here!"

Rags and David headed in.

"Whatever it was," Rags declared, "I didn't do it."

"Your sister did," Mrs. Kagan snapped. She stomped down the hall toward the kitchen.

Rags sprinted after her. David followed.

"Carrie didn't do nothin'," Rags said fiercely. "And if she did, I'm responsible for her."

Mrs. Kagan sniffed. "Miss Bradley, this is Carrie's brother, Rags."

Miss Bradley stood up and held out her hand to shake.

Rags scowled and took a step back. "Where's Carrie?"

Miss Bradley took a deep breath, as if she were so upset she was having trouble remembering to breathe. David knew that feeling.

"I don't know," she answered.

"What happened to my sister?"

"She ran away. . . ."

There had been a field trip for the class. The kids were supposed to get a permission slip signed by their parents in order to go. Carrie had forged the signature—"Mrs. Ragsdale."

"I told her she couldn't go without her mother's signature," Miss Bradley explained.

"We don't have a mother." Rags' hands balled into fists.

"I realize that now. This is all my fault. . . . I didn't know. . . . I didn't check the records."

"Carrie and I stayed up all night doing those stupid assignments." David didn't care if he sounded rude. "Didn't that count for anything?"

Miss Bradley nodded. "Yes, of course it did. I tried to telephone for permission, but there was no answer."

Mrs. Kagan's cheeks reddened. "I turned off the bell. *The Young and the Restless* was on. . . ."

"When I told her she couldn't go, she ran out of the school," Miss Bradley said. "I couldn't catch her. I hoped she'd come here."

"What about your exclusive field trip?" Rags snarled.

"The principal took it. We have to look for her."

"No thanks!" Rags shouted. "I can look after my own sister!"

He bolted out of the kitchen. The front door slammed.

Miss Bradley straightened her shoulders. "We can search the streets anyway. Mrs. Kagan, I can drive while you watch."

Mrs. Kagan stiffened, throwing a glance toward the living room where the TV droned. "That's impossible. I can't leave Mr. Kagan. Carrie'll get herself home when she's hungry. They always do."

"I'll come," David offered.

In the car, the teacher turned to him. "Where do you think she'd go?"

David shrugged. "A shopping center, maybe?"

Miss Bradley put the car in gear. They drove silently, up and down streets. At each strip mall David hopped out and combed the aisles of the stores. Nothing.

"What about North Central?" David suggested. "Maybe she went there, looking for Rags."

"Good idea." Miss Bradley wheeled the car in that direction. A few minutes later they stopped in front of the school. Carrie was nowhere in sight.

"I'll find Mr. McLeod," David said. "Rags does photography with him. Maybe she's there."

The teacher was alone in the photo lab—he hadn't seen Carrie. But he came outside to talk with Miss Bradley.

David looked up and down the street, wondering where Carrie could've gone. What if somebody hurt her?

"I'll get my car," said Mr. McLeod. "David'll have to

come with me, though. I'm not sure I'd recognize her."

"Wonderful! Thank you so much." Miss Bradley smiled.

Mr. McLeod reddened. "Glad to do it. They're good kids."

David followed Mr. McLeod to his shabby car. There were dents in the door and the vinyl seats were cracked, but the motor purred softly. The teacher shifted gears, and the car shot down the street.

"Did you try the city park?"

David shook his head.

Mr. McLeod took a left toward downtown. "That's where Rags took that last bunch of photos." He glanced at David. "Have you two become friends?"

David shrugged.

Mr. McLeod grimaced. "I know. Rags doesn't trust anyone."

The teacher turned in at the park entrance and drove slowly along the narrow road. David sat up and peered forward. "There they are!"

Rags was piggybacking Carrie along a path. The little girl clung to him, exhausted.

Mr. McLeod pulled up the car, got out, and waved. "Hey, Rags! How about a ride?"

Rags jogged over. Carrie clung to him, but he gently slid her around into the seat.

"I don't want to go to Mrs. Kagan's!" She began crying noisily, quickly rising to hysterics. Rags put his arms around her and, face flushed, glared at Mr. McLeod.

"David, have you seen the pond down this way?" The teacher opened the passenger door. "I'll show it to you."

David and Mr. McLeod walked around the pond for half an hour. His teacher asked him friendly questions about what he thought of school and where he was headed with his life. Even though he didn't say anything about David's dad, David had to struggle to answer. He used his best Lakethorn voice to say whatever he thought the teacher wanted to hear.

When David's stomach growled loudly Mr. McLeod led the way back to the car. Carrie was seat-belted but asleep. Rags sat facing out the open door.

"She okay?" the teacher asked.

Rags nodded. "Yeah. Thanks, Mr. McLeod.

"No problem."

They were back at the Kagans' in fifteen minutes. Miss Bradley had returned, too. She looked ready to cry with relief.

David headed up to his room and sprawled out on the bed. He batted a wadball back and forth between his hands.

Ten points . . . eleven . . . twelve . . . A clear pass through the defense line . . .

Outside he could hear the two teachers talking. They said good-bye several times and then their cars started up.

Footsteps sounded on the stairs. Through the open door David saw Rags carry his drowsy sister into her bedroom. Mrs. Kagan followed.

"And don't you be expecting me to go heat up some nice little dinner for you and David, Johnny Ragsdale."

Rags grunted.

"And that little girl had me worried half to death. Mr.

Kagan was so worn down over it, he couldn't eat his pork chop."

Give him milk and cookies, David thought.

Rags stomped downstairs. The front door slammed.

By the time the front door opened again David had scored nearly fifty points. His head thrummed with the roar of the crowd and the strains of the triumphal march.

The bedroom door banged wide open. Arms loaded with McDonald's bags, Rags stalked in. He tossed a bulging bag to David.

The roar of the crowed stopped.

Juicy mouthed with hunger, David ripped it open — two burgers, large fries, and an apple pie. Rags took a couple of shakes from the bag he carried and handed one to David.

"I owe you, man."

He took a bag into Carrie's bedroom, then came back and sprawled on the bed. A second later he'd pulled on his earphones and cranked up the music.

Clear across the room David could hear the vibrations. He smiled, slouched back on his own bed, and chowed down.

CHAPTER

9

Over the next few weeks David tore out of his last class and ran his fastest . . . keeping clear of Sean's gang . . . getting home before the delivery boy slung the newspaper onto the porch.

Scared stiff, he peeled through the paper daily, but there was never anything else about his father.

A week before Christmas, Mrs. Kagan had him and Rags haul an old artificial tree from the basement. There were only a few ornaments and they were chipped. No matter what they did, the angel that sat on top tipped over drunkenly.

"You know, Ma," Rags said thoughtfully. "I'd say that's a fallen angel."

"Don't start on me, Johnny Ragsdale," Mrs. Kagan snapped. "That's an antique tree topper."

"I can see that!" Rags agreed. "But if I were you, I'd check the beer bottles, 'cause if she ain't a fallen angel, she's a tipsy one."

He dodged a swat from Mrs. Kagan's rolled-up magazine and grinned.

Betty Joseph stuck her head into the room.

"Are you going to help decorate?" Carrie asked her.

Betty rolled her eyes. "That thing? No way. Besides, I got a date. See ya." She left.

Once the tree had been hung with the decorations, David stood looking at it for a long time. If he shut his eyes, he could remember the smell of pine from the years he and his mother had decorated their own Christmas tree. No matter how bad things were during the year, Christmas magic always remade their family. Even his father would get caught up in the holiday spirit when they went to choose their tree.

In the dark and frosty cold they'd scamper among the trees, breathing deep green smells, laughing at jokes about trees that were too tall or too wide, until finally they agreed that *this* one was perfect.

Last Christmas, a million years ago when his mother had still been alive, David and Mrs. Rizutto bought a tree from the gas station parking lot. His mother sat smiling, wrapped in a quilt in the big armchair, while David and the housekeeper strung garlands of stale popcorn and cranberries. His dad had said he was too busy at work.

"Mrs. Kagan," David said. "I'd like to make some popcorn-and-cranberry garlands for the tree."

"Not them food strings." Mrs. Kagan plunked herself on the sofa. "Brings on rats and mice. And spiders."

"'Not a creature was stirring, not even a mouse,'" Carrie recited dreamily from the foot of the tree.

"We always had garlands," David insisted, "and we never had rats or mice. I'll pay for the stuff myself."

"Hmph! Little Father Christmas, ain't you? Suppose you're going to want us to start singin' Christmas carols next."

Carrie spun around and jumped to her feet. "Can we?"

Her eyes sparkled, but as she saw Mrs. Kagan's aghast expression, her eyes dulled and her cheeks reddened.

"Sure, we can!" David said loudly. "While we string the popcorn."

Carrie smiled and settled back under the tree.

"Anything else?" Mrs. Kagan demanded. "Mr. Kagan in a Santa suit and climbin' down the chimney? Some reindeer for the yard? Just ask. It's Christmas, ain't it?"

"Bah, humbug!" Rags growled.

"I'll get the stuff tomorrow," David promised Carrie. She smiled up at him.

The next day he skipped a couple of classes and bought popcorn and a bag of cranberries. He didn't have much money left from the allowance he'd saved, but David recklessly spent it all on a baby doll for Carrie.

He grinned while he walked home. They were going to have Christmas, no matter what. He had a week to find gifts for everyone.

When he got home that night, there was a package and a card from Mrs. Rizutto.

OPEN NOW!!! was written all over the package.

While the rest of the family looked on, David ripped it open. Inside was a huge tin of homemade Christmas cookies—the kind he and his mother had made every year. David blinked at it. Carrie nudged him and looked up hopefully.

"Oh, wow!" Betty Joseph swooped down and grabbed a handful. "These are so fabulous!" she exclaimed through the crumbs. Her hand extended for more. David grabbed the tin.

"Carrie first!"

Wide-eyed, Carrie took one cookie with a cherry flower on top.

"Hmph. I would've thought I might deserve a cookie. I'm the one that feeds and clothes you all. . . ." Mrs. Kagan eyed the can greedily.

In a flash, Rags grabbed the can out of David's hands and darted to the other side of the kitchen.

"But, Ma! There's no milk and cookies for folks like us!"

"Johnny Ragsdale, so help me, I'll make you sorry you were born!"

Rags grinned and held the tin out of reach. "How could I be, with you for a Ma?"

"Rags!" Mrs. Kagan shrieked.

She took off after him. David, Betty, and Carrie laughed so hard they cried as Mrs. Kagan chased after Rags. Mr. Kagan glanced at them as they tore past his chair but then returned his eyes to the television.

Finally David wrested the cookies from Rags and with his best Lakethorn manners offered them to Mrs. Kagan.

"I'm only taking 'em because I deserve 'em," Mrs. Kagan announced. She took a bigger handful than Betty Joseph. "Thank you, David. Nice to have one gentleman in this house." She stalked off to the living room.

Rags shook his head. "Davey boy, you are full of it."

David grinned, took a cookie, and handed the tin to Carrie. While the other three happily munched, David opened the card. A twenty-dollar bill fell out.

"Oh, wow!" Betty said. "David, how about a loan?"

"In your dreams, Betty." David retrieved the money and read the card.

Dear David,

I think about you often. I have a good new job now, but my leg still hurts after the day is over. The Williamses have two boys and a girl, but the children are not nice like you. I try and teach them to be good and they learn to mind me.

Mrs. Williams does not like meatloaf or casseroles, but I teach her, too.

Do you grow big and strong now? I keep the nice card you send me on my dresser. I do not know what size you are, so I send you this to buy a present for you.

From your loving Mrs. Rizutto

David held the money tight, imagined new clothes or maybe a cheap tape player, then sighed.

There'd be no cards and cookies for the other three. So if they were all going to have a Christmas . . .

That night the kids sat around the kitchen table stringing cranberry-and-popcorn garlands. Mrs. Kagan sniffed about rats and mice but produced a small bowl of Christmas candies. Betty Joseph sang carols for Carrie.

It was the best fun David had had for months—since before his mother got sick. When he went to bed, he took out his mom's diary. He flipped through the pages to the same date two years ago—his last magic Christmas.

"Oh, tannenbaum!" We got our tree today. It's the best one ever. Tony says I say that every year. But seeing as it's the only time of year I can get him away from his business, it's the best—used to be like that with Dad, too.

Tony and David were laughing and giggling for about an hour trying to put the tree up. It kept falling over until both of them looked like wood elves—hair full of pine needles!

They did their annual hands-measuring thing. Palm to palm, the tips of David's fingers reached the top bend in Tony's. My little man is getting bigger all the time.

David closed the diary and lay back. He held up his hand and studied it. His fingers were long like his mom's. Probably his hand was as big as his dad's now.

The next day he cut school again to buy the rest of the presents.

At a secondhand bookstore, he bought a photography book for Rags. A bunch of free perfume samples from the department stores and a hair clip took care of Betty. After a lot of thought David picked out a scarf for Mrs. Kagan. He was stumped on what to get for Mr. Kagan, then finally settled on a box of candy. Mrs. Kagan would eat it all, but he wasn't sure Mr. Kagan would notice anyway.

That left him about two and a half dollars.

"Easy come, easy go." David shrugged.

He was so caught up in thinking about Christmas that he forgot to hurry back in time to intercept the newspaper.

By the time David remembered and ran the rest of the way, it was too late. The paper had already disappeared from the steps.

David swallowed and hurried up to his room to stash the presents. There wouldn't be anything in the paper today. Why should there be?

Maybe Mrs. Kagan hadn't started reading it yet. David raced downstairs.

In the kitchen, Betty Joseph was fixing a sandwich and

complaining loudly that she didn't get enough spending money. Mrs. Kagan ignored her, holding the newspaper up to read.

On the front page, facing David across the table, was his father's photograph.

The headline read: FUGITIVE ARRESTED.

David felt as though the air were thrumming. He opened his mouth, then shut it again.

"Mrs. Kagan, it isn't fair!" Betty Joseph repeated. "Even the kids whose families are on welfare get more money than me. . . ."

"Mrs. Kagan . . ." David's voice sounded odd even to himself.

Mrs. Kagan lowered the paper and looked at him.

She knows, David thought wildly.

"I mean, jeez, you don't want me to do drug runs, do ya?"

Mrs. Kagan's eyes were brusquely sympathetic.

"Could I . . . see the paper?"

Mrs. Kagan folded the pages and handed them to David.

"Oh yeah, right!" Betty Joseph declared. "I have a serious problem, but who cares? Nobody! David gets the Christmas cookies. David gets the twenty bucks. . . ." She stomped out of the room, shouting over her shoulder, "Everything's easy for David. . . . It isn't fair!"

David barely heard her. He stared down at the photo of his father: FUGITIVE ARRESTED.

*

CHAPTER

10

David held the newspaper with numb fingers. There was his dad's photo staring out at him—at the whole world. Mrs. Kagan watched him, frowning.

"Could I . . . could I keep this?"

She nodded.

"Thank you." Like a robot David went up to his bedroom. He couldn't make himself read the article, so finally he stashed the paper under the mattress.

Still on automatic, David ripped a sheet from a notebook and crumpled up a ball. With one smooth stroke he whacked the ball into the air.

. . . *David Borelli . . . wadball champion . . . champion of the world . . . the greatest champion . . . anywhere . . . anytime . . .*

The crowd roared. David tore around the room, driving the ball higher and higher, whacking it harder and harder, until, exhausted, he fell on his bed.

He didn't know how he made it through dinner. Betty Joseph chattered about her new boyfriend. Rags goaded her into shouting. Eyes wide, Carrie watched. David put one forkful of stew after another into his mouth.

"Oh, that's enough, Betty," Mrs. Kagan said sharply.

"Nobody ever listens to what I say." Betty sulked.

"Seems we never hear anything else." Mrs. Kagan put down her coffee cup. "Carrie, if you clear off the dishes real quick, you kids could make a batch of Christmas cookies."

They stared at their foster mother in disbelief. Carrie's eyes slowly grew wider, and she grinned.

"Did a reindeer bite you?" Rags asked.

"Don't you start, Johnny Ragsdale," Mrs. Kagan snapped. "It's Christmas, ain't it?"

"All right!" Betty Joseph cheered.

As she left the table Mrs. Kagan turned to David. "Now, David, you take charge. I'm countin' on you."

She poured herself one more cup of coffee and went into the living room with Mr. Kagan.

They argued over what kind of cookies to make. Rags would've stormed off except for Carrie's tears. In the end they made star-shaped sugar cookies and shortbread that baked into rock-hard circles.

Even David found himself laughing as a poof of flour coated Betty Joseph's face.

When the boys got into bed, the newspaper crackled under David's mattress. He froze, afraid Rags would hear. But his roommate just yawned loudly, then rolled over with the blankets heaped over his head.

David lay still for ages, listening to his heart thudding and Rags' breathing. At last he eased out of bed, groped under the mattress, and headed to the bathroom.

It was a long time before he could unglue his eyes from the photograph and the headline: FUGITIVE ARRESTED.

Finally he read the article. It didn't say much—only that his father had been caught in another city and was being sent back. Then the article repeated all the charges.

David leaned back against the cold toilet tank and gulped deep breaths, but the tears came out anyway.

The bathroom door opened. Carrie, eyes practically closed, stumbled in. She squinted at David, then sleepily rubbed the wet from his cheeks.

"I gotta go . . . ," she mumbled.

David left. He stashed the paper and sagged into bed. The toilet flushed. The hall light went out. The Kagans' bathroom was the only place to be in the middle of the night.

The next day David tried to cut school right after attendance, but Thin Lips was prowling the hall, watching the exits. In gym Mr. McLeod took out a big bag of soccer balls and started the boys kicking goals between fluorescent plastic cones.

David sidled in late, hoping no one would notice him.

Mr. McLeod motioned for him to line up for his turn to kick. David's breath was ragged, as if he'd been running. Sean was joking around with his buddies. He barely glanced David's way.

Nobody knows, David realized. He felt light-headed with relief. No one had seen the picture or the article.

He was safe!

The rush of relief turned sour. David's fists clenched and his shoulders shook. He wanted to pound someone. Anyone. It wasn't fair! None of this was fair.

Thwack!

He kicked the soccer ball so hard it shot between the goals, ricocheted off the wall, and walloped Sean in the head. The bully spun around.

Mr. McLeod grinned. "Keep your attention on what's happening, Moskovitz. It's safer."

Most of the guys snickered. Rags smoothly pulled David into the middle of the line. Sean glowered, rubbed the back of his head, and looked around for whoever'd kicked the ball. No one said anything.

"You're holding up the line, Moskovitz. Move it!" Mr. McLeod commanded. Sean glowered and kicked.

"Looking for an early funeral, Davey boy?" Rags grinned.

"Good shot, Borelli," Grif said out of the side of his mouth. He eyed the ball, swung his long leg, and missed.

He swore.

"Albert, are you going out for soccer this year?" Mr. McLeod asked.

"Yes, sir!"

"I was afraid of that."

Grif grinned and kicked again. This time he connected with the ball, but it whumped against the wall without much force.

"Borelli," Grif said over his shoulder, "how'd you do that?"

David shrugged and grinned. After that it wasn't so hard to get through the day.

But two days later the newspaper printed another article about his father. It said all the old stuff but this time added that bail had been set at a million dollars. Anthony Borelli was being held at the county jail.

From then on David cut classes whenever he could.

The vice principal yanked him into his office for a lecture about his attitude. David didn't even bother using his Lakethorn voice.

The crowds roared. . . . Three hundred goals scored by David Borelli, wadball champion of the universe . . .

Mrs. Kagan threatened to cut off his allowance if he didn't stop crashing around his room. Rags promised to tear David's arms off if he slammed into his bed one more time.

On Christmas Day, David felt like a robot, smiling, giving the presents he'd chosen. Carrie sighed and lifted the doll into her arms as though it were a real baby.

"Oh, this is gorgeous!" Betty Joseph daubed herself with perfume that smelled awful and danced around with the hair clip twisting back her hair. Impulsively, she hugged David.

Rags held his nose and grinned. Then he ripped the wrappings off the parcel David handed him. His smile faded. He flipped through the book, then put it aside.

"Let's see that doll, Carrie." He reached for Carrie and drew her, squealing, into a bear hug.

David looked on in surprise. He'd thought Rags would get really excited about the photography book. With much noise and show, Mrs. Kagan hung the scarf around her neck and then tore open Mr. Kagan's candy.

David opened the new jeans and T-shirt from Mrs. Kagan and the used soccer ball from Rags.

Did prisoners at the county jail get presents at Christmas? Could they send them?

Carrie gave him a lumpy package and watched while he pulled off the wrappings. A school-project clay pot nestled inside. Red and green M&Ms spilled out of it. David let the candies slip onto his palms, until Carrie's anxious face finally snapped him awake.

"It's great, Carrie," he told her. She smiled hugely and hugged the doll against her chest.

That afternoon, while Mrs. Kagan napped and Rags blasted his ears with a new tape, David slipped out of the house and walked to a phone booth at the gas station.

His hands were shaking when he dialed the number of the jail. A receptionist answered.

"Hello," David said. He had to keep his Lakethorn voice. He had to. "Could I speak to Anthony Borelli, please? He's . . . he's staying there."

There was a brief pause. "I'm sorry, but the prisoners are not allowed to receive telephone calls."

"I wanted to say Merry Christmas. It's . . . it's his son calling."

Again the pause. As if the woman were thinking things she couldn't say.

"I'm sorry." Pause. "You could write him a letter and ask him to call you. Does he have your number?"

"No. No, he doesn't."

The voice sounded relieved. "Then why don't you write and put in your phone number? Do you want the address?"

"Please, yes . . ." David dug for a pencil. When the woman recited the address over the phone, David scribbled it on the paper with the jail's phone number.

"Thank you." David managed.

"You're welcome. And Merry Christmas."

"Yeah, Merry Christmas."

That night in the bathroom he wrote a letter to his dad. It sounded simple-minded— Was his dad okay? He was fine. Please, would he call . . .

A week later, when there'd been no phone call, David wrote another letter.

Even though it was vacation, David hung around the house, certain he'd miss the call if he went out.

There was no call.

The day before vacation was over Scott showed up again. David realized he'd never hated anyone in his life, except for maybe Sean, the way he hated his volunteer.

"The court date for the dependency hearing's a week from Wednesday," Scott told him.

"So?" David grunted.

"Do you want to be there?"

"What's the point?"

Scott gripped David's shoulder. "I know it's tough, but with your dad in custody, this is the best way."

"Sure." David jerked his shoulder away. He walked out of the kitchen, out of the house, and ran until he could barely breathe. When he stumped back two hours later Scott had gone.

Vacation was over. David drifted from class to class. On Friday he blew it—Sean and his buddies caught him in the washroom.

"This is gettin' old, man," Grif protested.

"He's dead, an' I'm the executioner," Sean gloated.

Grif shook his head and walked out. That left four against one. David fought furiously and escaped with a bloody nose and aching ribs. When Rags saw him in the halls he just walked away.

That night, holding a cold cloth on his bruises, David realized he had to get his head together. He had to see his dad.

The next day was Saturday. David got up early and dressed in his Lakethorn clothes. Rags sat on the bed, camera cradled between his knees as he adjusted and readjusted the settings.

"You got a hot date?"

David didn't answer. He left the room and went downstairs, easing out the front door quietly. Once outside he jogged through the slush to the bus stop.

He stamped his feet to keep warm until the bus rolled up. David paid his fare and sank into a seat near the front.

White knuckled, he watched unfamiliar streets go past. First shabby neighborhoods, then huge Old Belmont mansions, then, as the bus swung toward the city center, blocks of shops and businesses.

David checked and rechecked the address even though he knew it by heart. And then it was his stop. The doors opened and David stepped out onto the sidewalk.

The jail loomed before him.

CHAPTER

11

The gray stone county jail was massive. A woman and a teenage girl went in. David followed.

Inside, David stood watching, unsure what to do. Ahead was a metal door frame—a detector like one at an airport. A guard stood beside it, rocking on his heels, looking bored.

The woman and girl went through. It beeped for the girl. Grumbling, she took off her necklace—a thin steel chain with all kinds of stuff hanging from it—and dropped it onto the tray the guard held out.

"I don't see why you can't fix this so it only goes off for guns or knives or something. Jeez!" She went through the gate again.

David took a deep breath and walked through. It didn't beep. He avoided looking at the guard and went up to the receptionist seated behind a big glass window.

Bulletproof, David thought.

The woman and girl filled out slips of paper and passed

them through a slot in the glass. The woman slid her driver's license through, too. The girl smiled at David.

The receptionist examined the woman's slip. "Fill in your relationship to the prisoner, please." She slid the paper back out.

"Oh . . ." The woman hesitated. "I'm his girlfriend, y'know? And this is my daughter."

"Write that in," the receptionist told her.

The woman scribbled on the slip and gave it back.

The receptionist typed something into a computer and waited a moment, then returned the driver's license. "Up the stairs to your right and see the receptionist in the lobby."

The woman and girl left. David went to the window.

"I . . . I'd like to visit someone, please. . . ."

The woman looked him over. "Is your mom here with you?"

"No . . . I . . . she can't . . ."

"Your dad, then?"

David swallowed. He couldn't say the words.

The woman nodded, understanding. "You'll have to come back with your legal guardian. Kids can't visit prisoners without their parent or guardian with them."

Red faced, determined not to cry, David retreated. Outside he smacked the stone wall with his hand. Somewhere in there his father was sitting in a cell and somehow David had to see him.

When he got to the Kagans', Miss Bradley's car was parked in front. She and Carrie were saying good-bye as David went in.

"Get those wet shoes off before you mess up my nice floor," Mrs. Kagan snapped.

David sat on the stairs and struggled with the wet knots of his sneakers. Mrs. Kagan returned her attention to the teacher.

"You ain't gettin' paid to spend all this out-of-school time with Carrie," Mrs. Kagan probed.

Miss Bradley looked down at the child clasping her hand. "Carrie's special."

Mrs. Kagan looked her foster daughter over. "Hmm. Is she, now?"

Miss Bradley just swung Carrie's hand slightly and smiled. Carrie smiled back. "Mr. McLeod and I are going to see a movie tomorrow. If it's all right with Mrs. Kagan, would you and your brother like to come? Our treat."

Carrie beamed and nodded.

"You're invited, too, David," Miss Bradley added.

David assumed his Lakethorn smile and voice. "Thank you, but I'm visiting some friends tomorrow."

Mrs. Kagan frowned. "You'll get these kids expecting treats that ain't likely to happen. It'll hurt 'em, Miss Bradley."

"I won't hurt her," Miss Bradley replied. "I'll come about one, Carrie."

The door closed. David got the last knot untied. Carrie cradled her doll and wandered past him up the stairs, singing softly. Mrs. Kagan set her hands on her hips and scowled at David.

"Nice of you to show up, your lordship. Hungry, are you? And I s'pose it's too much for the hired help to ask where your lordship's been all day?"

David picked up his shoes and set them neatly on the rubber mat against the wall.

"I went downtown."

"Downtown? He went downtown! And did what? Visited the mayor? Did you tell him that the money I get for you kids won't keep us from starvation? And that I wear my heart out worryin' about you all!"

David grinned. "Sorry, Ma! But I was looking into a life of crime and I didn't want you to fuss."

Her mouth twitched. "You're as bad as that Johnny Ragsdale, and he's no good. Now, what's this about visiting friends tomorrow?"

David thought quickly. The idea had been hovering there anyway. "Mrs. Rizutto asked me to come over."

"When did she do that?"

"Last week. Remember, I told you all about it."

Mrs. Kagan snorted. "So now I'm senile! Well, you been too good to be true since you got here, David. Just you see you don't get into more'n you can handle."

She went back to the kitchen. David retrieved his shoes.

Once again he closed the door quietly and jogged down the street toward the phone booth. The phone rang four times before someone picked it up.

"Hello?"

"Hello . . . Mrs. Rizutto? It's David."

"David! Everything is all right with you?"

David took a shaky breath. "No. Not really. Did you see the paper? My father . . . Dad was arrested."

There was a pause. "My boy Joe read it to me. Do you want me to come for you? Do you need my boys to come and help you?"

"Mrs. Rizutto, I have to go see him. They won't let me in without an adult."

"Pah! That man was not good enough for your mother

and not for you either. You do better to let him stay in jail and forget about him."

"He's my father."

"You're just like your mama. She say to me, 'Mrs. Rizutto, he's my husband.' I say 'that doesn't make him a good man.' "

David took a deep breath. "I have to see him."

There was another long pause. "David, I do not think seeing your papa is a good idea. He's not a good papa. He's not like you and your mama."

David waited. Mrs. Rizutto sighed.

"Your mama was the same. I say no to her, then somehow I do what she wants. When do you want to do this?"

"Tomorrow."

She hesitated so long that David was afraid she would refuse after all.

"David, you are good like your mama. But like your papa you take foolish chances." She sighed. "Where shall I meet you?"

That night David felt almost feverish with excitement and dread. He slept, yelped himself awake from frantic dreams, and lay twisted in the sheets, sweating as though he'd run a long, long way.

As soon as light streaked his window he was up and dressed.

There was a fast-food place near the school. David headed for it, ordered some breakfast, and sat in a booth where someone had left a newspaper. He ate slowly, tasting nothing, going through page after page to see if there was anything about his father. Not today.

He caught the bus downtown.

David walked up and down the block. Finally another

bus lumbered into sight. The doors opened, and Mrs. Rizutto got off.

David hugged her fiercely. She hugged back. "There, there, my David. I come, just like I say I do."

Feeling stupid, David pulled away. She looked at him closely.

"Yes, I think you grow," Mrs. Rizutto pronounced. "You get bigger and you get stronger. I feel it in your hug. Maybe you do sports at your new school?"

David felt his face heat up. She smiled expectantly.

"Track," he said. "I do a lot of running."

"Good, good! So where is it we go to see your papa? What do we say?"

David pointed down the street to the looming gray building. "Over there." They started walking. "I'm going to say I'm your son, okay?"

"You want me to say I'm your mama, Marie Borelli?"

"No," David explained. "You say you're Dad's girl-friend. . . ."

"Mr. Rizutto would not like that," she interrupted.

David took a deep breath. "He won't know! I can say I'm your son—David Rizutto. They won't check my ID, so they'll let us in. I saw some other people do that."

Mrs. Rizutto frowned but kept walking. "You're just like your mama, making me do things I think I should not."

"What did Mom make you do?" David tried to change the subject.

"That is between her and me. I keep my word, but I think she was wrong." Mrs. Rizutto looked down at David. "Your foster mother, is she good to you, David?"

"She's okay."

"You get lots to eat? Good food, so you grow big and strong?"

David smiled. "You said I'm bigger and stronger."

She put her arm around his shoulders and squeezed. "I would like for you to be happy, too, David, but I guess that is a lot for now, eh?'

"I guess."

They reached the steps. Mrs. Rizutto clutched her purse nervously but walked determinedly to the door. She hesitated before the metal detector, then handed over her purse and walked through.

David followed and pointed to the receptionist. Mrs. Rizutto marched over to the window.

"I am Mrs. Rizutto," she announced. "I wish to see my . . . boyfriend, Anthony Borelli."

David held his breath. The receptionist gave them forms to fill out. David wrote "David Rizutto" and slipped it through the slot. Mrs. Rizutto looked the paper over and filled in her name and address and all the other information asked for; then she put her form through the slot, too.

"Could I see your driver's license, please?"

"I do not drive," Mrs. Rizutto said.

David's mouth went dry. His heart hammered.

"Do you have other ID?" the receptionist asked.

Mrs. Rizutto carefully took out a plastic card and put it through the slot.

The woman typed something into the computer, then returned the card. "Please check in with the receptionist in the lobby upstairs to your right."

"Thank you," Mrs. Rizutto said.

Together she and David went up. The lobby upstairs had plastic chairs, vending machines, and another receptionist sitting behind a wall of glass. This time they filled out a pink slip. David clenched and unclenched his fists. While they waited for the receptionist, Mrs. Rizutto bought herself a cup of coffee and a chocolate bar for David.

"I'm not really hungry," he said.

"Eat," she told him. "You need the energy it gives you."

David shook his head and shoved the bar into his pocket. The receptionist called them over and slid two passes through the slot in the window.

"Take the elevator to the eighth floor," she told them.

As they rode upward David tried to think about what he would say to his dad. The doors whooshed open before he could decide.

The elevator opened into a big room. On one side was a row of booths. Each booth had a plastic chair, a telephone receiver on one side, and a back wall made of thick glass. In three of the booths people talked on the telephones to prisoners on the other side of the glass.

Mrs. Rizutto showed their passes to a guard. David just stood there.

Behind the glass wall he could see a guard escorting his father to a booth.

CHAPTER

12

Mrs. Rizutto put her hand on David's shoulder and gently pushed him toward the booth. On the other side his father joked with the guard, then sat down in the seat facing them.

Even in the red prisoner's jumpsuit, his dad seemed the same. He was thinner and had bags under his eyes, but as always Anthony Borelli looked around as though he were in charge of everything.

He winked at David and picked up the phone on his side. When David just stood there, his father smiled as if this were a joke they shared and tapped the receiver.

David sat down and picked up his end.

"Dad? Hi!"

The voice that came through was tinny, but it was his father. "Hello, David. What a surprise!"

"I wanted to see you. Make sure you're okay."

"You don't have to worry about me, David. I know how to look after myself."

David grinned. "Never show 'em you're scared."

His dad grinned back. "That's right. Do they treat you all right in the foster home?"

"Yeah. It's okay. They wouldn't let Mrs. Rizutto take me. She doesn't have enough room." David hesitated. "Why didn't you answer my letters?"

"Because I thought it would be better for you to forget about me and make your own life."

"Mom said family has to stick together, no matter what. If family isn't loyal, there's no family." David blinked hard.

"Your mom was right. But I don't need loyalty. I need about fifty thousand for my legal fees." He smiled ruefully. "If there was a way for you to help me, David, I'd tell you. You just keep up your school work and get on with your life. Your mom would want that."

"Is that what you want?"

"It's what's best for us both."

"I guess." David swallowed. "Scott, the volunteer the court sent, told me they're having my dependency hearing next week. He's a real jerk, but he tells me about all the court dates."

"Whoa." David's dad leaned closer to the window. "What court dates?"

"You know. You aren't around, so they're making me a ward of the state."

"They can't do that without my consent!"

"Scott says they can and there's nothing we can do about it."

"Don't count on it, son." He leaned closer to the glass and his eyes glinted. "There's always something that can be done."

"Like what?"

Borelli grinned. "You just get on with your life, but in the meantime you rely on your old man."

"Yeah, well. I guess I'd better go."

David stood up and turned to leave. Abruptly he turned back and placed his palm on the glass. Their eyes met, and then his dad laid his palm against the glass, too. David's hand was narrower, but his fingertips stretched just above his father's.

The guard came over, touched Anthony Borelli's elbow, and gestured toward the door to the cells.

Mrs. Rizutto put her arm around David's shoulders and guided him toward the elevator. David craned his neck to look back, just as his father did the same.

The elevator opened. Three people got out. David and Mrs. Rizutto got in.

Out on the street Mrs. Rizutto put her hands on his shoulders. "Are you all right, my David? Do you want to go have hot chocolate?"

David shook his head. "No. I . . . I have homework. . . ."

"Good," Mrs. Rizutto nodded approvingly. "You do well in your studies. That is what your mama would have wanted."

David pulled away. "I have to get my bus."

"You phone Mrs. Rizutto if you need anything," she called after him.

He sprinted through the slush to the stop on the other side of the street. A moment later his bus came around the corner.

Once in a seat David stared at the jail. Maybe his dad didn't really steal all that money. A good lawyer could prove he was innocent, and then they wouldn't need a dependency hearing.

The bus lurched. David gripped the seat ahead. Where

would his father ever get the money to pay a good lawyer?

The bus stopped. David slogged through the slush toward the Kagans' house, reaching it just as Miss Bradley and Mr. McLeod came out. Rags and Carrie followed.

"C'mon, guys," Mr. McLeod said, "or we'll miss the second movie, too."

"David." Miss Bradley greeted him. "You're just in time!"

"And we're late," Mr. McLeod reminded her.

"We're going to get popcorn and drinks!" Carrie exclaimed.

They insisted that David come. He didn't have the energy to argue. Once there, the images filled his mind, blotting out everything else. Rags shot popcorn at a couple of cute girls until Mr. McLeod told him to knock it off. Carrie sat up wide-eyed, shrieking at the funny parts, crying at the sad ones.

Afterward they ate in a fast-food place with a lot of other families. By the time Mr. McLeod and Miss Bradley dropped them off, Carrie was in seventh heaven, laughing and giggling.

"Hmm," Mrs. Kagan said. "If I'd known a movie'd make you such a happy little thing, I might've sent you myself."

Carrie hugged her and danced upstairs.

That night, while David got ready for bed, Rags spent a few minutes looking at papers taken from a big brown envelope Mr. McLeod had given him.

David shut his eyes. . . . *David Borelli . . . champion of the world . . . stands before a cheering crowd of hundreds of thousands*. The picture faded into nightmares. He tossed around all night.

The next day David couldn't wake up. When Thin Lips

gave him a week of detentions for missed assignments, David thanked him; the vice principal slapped him with Saturday school for smart-mouthing.

David forgot about it immediately. After school, when he passed by the photo lab, Mr. McLeod was chewing Rags out. David scowled and kept going. Rags'd have McLeod wrapped around his little finger in three minutes.

David walked slowly out of the school and down the street.

"Hey, butthead!"

David wheeled around. Sean and his gang had trailed him from the Mini-Mart.

David threw his books on the grass. He'd kill them!

"Eat my socks, pig breath!" David screamed.

In two seconds they were on him. David punched and kicked and swore, but it was four to one. When they got tired of pounding him, Sean dumped David on the grass.

"So long, butthead! Same time tomorrow!"

David sprawled face-down, swearing into the grass. Blood dripped from his nose and a cut above his eye. It hurt to breathe. If he could die soon, David thought, it would be a good thing.

But he didn't die. So he got up, collected his books, and started walking. At home David headed directly for the bathroom to press a cold cloth against his face. Betty Joseph rattled upstairs and stopped before the open door. "You guys think you're so-o-o macho. Are you bleeding to death?"

"No."

"Then don't drip blood on the bath mat. Mrs. Kagan'll kill you and I'll have to wash it."

"Thanks for the sympathy."

David threw the washcloth into the tub, went into his room, and flopped onto the bed. He shut his eyes to the dingy room. He faintly heard the distant roar of the crowd. They were chanting . . .

Borelli! Borelli! Borelli! David Borelli . . . wadball champion of the world. The crowd cheers—Borelli stands alone. . . .

In a smooth motion David stood up. He crumpled the paper into a crackling ball and tossed it into the air.

Borelli! Borelli! Borelli!

He would be okay. The other team was winning, but Borelli was on the field now. He was small, but he was fast . . . and he never gave up! Never! The crowds cheered all evening.

But when he dropped exhausted into bed later, it went wrong.

. . . on the podium . . . David Borelli . . . champion . . . no cheers . . . The crowd's after him. . . . He runs and runs . . . . The ground tips and he falls . . . tumbling over and over down a hill. . . . Sean grabs him. . . . Dad smiles and writes checks that float in the air. . . . His mom is there . . . farther and farther away . . . behind the glass wall. . . .

David screamed and screamed and then woke up.

He was breathing hard, sweating. How loud had he yelled? The heap of blankets on Rags' bed didn't move.

After about ten minutes of tossing around, David rolled out of bed and went to the bathroom. Light shone under the door. He could just make out Carrie's voice.

He sighed. Another middle-of-the-night party in the Kagans' bathroom. Just what he needed.

David tapped softly. "Carrie, it's me—David. You okay?"

She yanked the door wide, relief shining in her eyes.

"Carrie, *no!*" Rags hissed. He crouched on the floor, papers spread out in front and an open dictionary beside him. He slammed the dictionary shut and stood up, glaring at David. "Get out of here, Borelli!"

Carrie slid between them. "David will help," she pleaded.

David returned Rags' angry look and stepped into the bathroom. "Sure, I'll help you with your homework, Carrie. Is it too tough for Rags?"

Carrie grabbed Rags' clenched fist and pushed him back. "It's not my homework. It's a photo contest. See." She pointed to a printed application form. Rags snatched it off the floor.

"Carrie, shut up!" he growled.

"No. Mr. McLeod said you have to." She looked at David. "Rags can't fill it out."

"Try reading the directions," David said scornfully.

"But he can't read . . ." Carrie started.

"Carrie!" Rags looked like somebody'd sucker-punched him. His breath came hard and his face flushed red. "I told you to shut up!"

"You can't read?" David repeated, bewildered. And now he understood why Rags had been so weird about the photography book.

"Of course I can read! I'm not stupid!" Rags ripped up the application form and threw the pieces on the floor. "I don't care what McLeod says. I don't want to enter the stupid contest!"

He pushed past David and went into his room.

"Carrie, why can't Rags read?" David asked.

The girl shrugged. "'Cause of Mama. She did lots of

drugs, so she never remembered to feed me. I would've died, 'cept Rags looked after me."

"But why can't Rags read?"

Carrie scowled. "He couldn't take a baby to school, could he? And he couldn't leave me alone. So he didn't go. When we got put in a foster home, they sent Rags to school every single day. 'Cept by then all the kids knew how to read an' he didn't. They made fun of him, so he beat 'em all up. Now he's bad," she said with simple pride, "so nobody ever guesses."

Carrie took David's hand. "I told him you'd help."

He jerked his hand away. "Forget it, Carrie. I've got problems of my own."

He went back to bed.

CHAPTER

13

David pulled the covers over his head.

The roar of the crowd . . . the cheers rise higher and higher. . . . And then David Borelli, champion wadball player of the world, walks onto the field. . . .

Footsteps padded across the floor. David opened one eye. Carrie put all the papers on Rags' dresser, then softly padded out again.

The roar of the crowd died. David stuffed the pillow into his mouth. Sean's gang was going to keep beating him up. His dad was going to prison. The court judge was going to rule that he didn't belong to any family. He was never . . .

There was a thump from across the room. David's eyes flew open. On the other side of the room, Rags was thrashing around in his own blankets. He wasn't sleeping too well either.

David sat up. "I won't tell anyone," he said.

The thrashing stopped. There was no answer.

David switched on the light. "Rags, I'll help you do the contest application."

Rags rolled over and sat up. "I don't need your help!"

"The hell you don't!" David told him. "We can make a deal."

"What kind of deal?" Rags eyed him suspiciously.

David pictured Sean bruised and bleeding under Rags' experienced fists. It was a very good picture. David sighed. His own fists pounding Sean would be even better.

"When I get back at Sean, will you back me up?"

"Waste him, you mean?"

David thought about Rags beating Sean to his knees. He shook his head. "No. Nobody's going to dump on me anymore. I'm going to get him myself—somehow. But I'll need backup."

"You'll need an ambulance." Rags untangled himself from his blankets. "I could do this application, y'know. I'm not stupid."

"I know."

"I just never entered a contest before." He picked up the papers, handed them to David, and sat on the bed. "McLeod gave me extra copies."

"No sweat." David pointed to the questions and read them aloud as if he needed to double-check the information.

At first Rags acted as if he didn't care; then at last he fixed his eyes hungrily on the paper.

David was yawning widely when he finally finished printing the last of the information about Rags. He shoved the paper at his roommate and indicated a line at the bottom. "Sign it here, then mail it with three photos. Put your name on the back of the photos."

"Thanks, Davey boy. I owe ya, man." Rags held the paper with both hands.

David got back onto his own bed and on impulse took his mother's diary and opened it near the front.

I can't believe it! I am really and truly going to have a baby. Tony is as excited as I am. He says I should tell Dad as a peacemaking gesture. Tony thinks Dad's influence could set him up again after the investment mess. If he knew my father like I do, he'd realize that Robert Gilman doesn't forget—or ever forgive. And neither does his daughter! I'll do almost anything for Tony—but not that. My child won't grow up under Dad's golden thumb. Money isn't that important.

David reread the entry. His grandfather's name was Robert Gilman. And it sounded as if he'd had a lot of money. But what had happened to make his mom hate her father? David couldn't remember her being mean to anyone. And she was the one who taught him that, above all, family had to stick together. It just didn't make sense.

And it didn't seem real, either. David yawned. The entry was almost fourteen years old. His grandfather must have died after that. Any money his mom inherited must be all gone by now—his dad would have spent it.

The next morning David hadn't even finished his cereal when the doorbell rang.

"Drat," Mrs. Kagan muttered. "Can't anybody wait till a decent hour to bring bad news?"

She stomped down the hall and a moment later came back with Scott.

"Well, now you've done it," he told David.

David stared at him over his cornflakes. Rags eyed the

volunteer as he poured himself a huge bowlful.

"Done what?" David asked.

"Your father has demanded and received a court-appointed lawyer to protest the dependency hearing."

"Cool," Rags said.

"Not cool," Scott declared. David noticed that when his face turned red like that, his mustache looked like a tuft of dog hair. "It doesn't change anything," he went on. "All this means is that there's another delay and valuable court and lawyer time are wasted."

"My dad is fighting for me?" David demanded.

Scott let his breath out. "Yes. I suppose you could look at it that way," he admitted. "But it'll take weeks—maybe months—and the outcome will be the same! Legal proceedings cost a lot of money. The court will try to charge your father for the expense, but because of his situation he'll never have to pay a cent."

"Congratulations, Davey boy," Rags said. "You are getting the benefit of our great country's resources. That's why we pay taxes."

Mrs. Kagan's mouth twitched. "Rags, if you're late for school again, Mr. Thelps'll kick you out, and you'll never get to pay them taxes."

"Aw, Ma," Rags said. "A swell guy like me? C'mon, Davey boy. We got a court system to support."

It was as if his brain had clicked on again. His dad was fighting for him!

In classes, David watched Sean and his gang.

Just you wait, pig breath, David gloated silently. I say the word, and Rags'll rip your guts out of your throat.

Later, as he ran home, he thought about the dependency trial. His dad had said he could do something, and he did. David slowed down. But what if he lost? What if his dad lost his own trial and went to jail? Scott was right. David would still be declared a ward of the state and he'd stay at Mrs. Kagan's. Could his dad's lawyer be smart enough to keep that from happening?

That night Rags tried again to talk him into playing on the school soccer team.

"No way," David told him.

"Davey boy, you'll miss playing with the school's top athlete!" Rags flexed his muscles in front of the mirror on their bedroom door. "God, I'm great!"

David made gagging noises. Rags tackled him and they rolled over and over on the floor until Mrs. Kagan stomped upstairs and yelled at them both.

But a couple of weeks later, as David headed out from classes into the late winter sunshine, Rags intercepted him.

"Soccer practice started last week."

"So?"

"McLeod said you gotta play on the team."

David tried to push him aside. "I don't have to do anything."

Rags grinned and didn't budge. "Davey boy, McLeod says you do. And I say you do. I saw you kick that soccer ball into Moskovitz's head. An' I live with you slammin' around the room whacking a ball of paper. The North Central Soccer Shockers needs you. I want to win a game this year."

"No way. I'm terrible at sports. At my other school I always got picked last. And I've got things to do."

David tried to walk away, but Rags lunged, got him in a headlock, and dragged him choking and struggling down the hall to the boys' locker room. He didn't let go until they were inside.

"Hey, Mr. McLeod," Rags yelled. "Guess what! Davey's joining the Shockers!"

"Good man!" McLeod slapped David on the back.

David was too busy gasping for air to say anything. The coach tossed him a team T-shirt.

"Okay, boys, let's move it!"

McLeod started them with warm-up drills. Then they practiced passing the ball to each other using the sides of their feet. David couldn't get it right. It was just like the Lakethorn teams—he was terrible at sports. What was he doing here?

"Borelli," Ryan sneered, "this is the boys' team. You play like a girl."

Thwack! David whammed the ball with his foot. It shot down the field and whanged against the fence. Breathing hard, David glared at Ryan triumphantly.

Grif's laugh brayed out. "Hey, man, you better try it the girl's way."

"Eat dirt!" Ryan slammed him.

"Okay, that's it." McLeod pulled the boys apart. "Ryan, hit the showers. Tomorrow you act like a member of the team or you're out."

Ryan balled his fists, but when he met McLeod's eyes, he backed down. "This team stinks anyway."

He stalked away.

"Mr. McLeod." Ralph Kopowski automatically pulled his T-shirt down over his big stomach. "Ryan's the only decent player we got!"

"You got me!" Rags declared.

The coach shrugged. "We don't need anyone who isn't a team player. Remember that, Ralph—and you, too, Rags.

Grif, set up the next drill. Let's go!"

They practiced more drills; then McLeod had half the boys take off their T-shirts. David, Rags, and Grif were "skins." Rags took center forward. McLeod directed David to his right. Grif was on the left.

They played for nearly an hour. Whenever he got the ball, no matter where he was on the field, Rags kicked it toward the goal. Most of the time it went wide.

"Make it easy, why don'tcha!" Ralph taunted from the goal.

"Bring it up!" McLeod shouted. "Pass to your team-mates!"

Rags ignored him.

"Rags!" David shouted furiously when Rags missed yet another shot. "You're giving away the goals!"

"Eat my dirt, Davey boy!" Rags roared up the field and made another wide kick.

Ralph picked up the ball and threw it way down the field. David controlled it with his knee.

"Pass it!" Rags shouted.

"Eat *my* dirt!" David kneed the ball into the air. His skin stung from the impact. The ball hit the ground. David dribbled with his feet. He could do it! His muscles, strengthened by weeks of running home, could handle the weight of the soccer ball. And the moves were just like wadball!

When one of the "shirts" bore down on him, David passed the ball to Grif. Miraculously, Grif controlled it with his knee.

Rags paced them, yelling, "Lemme get a shot!"

They were still halfway down the field.

"Not yet!" David called.

Two shirts raced toward Grif. He looked around wildly.

"Kick it!" Rags shoved aside a defender.

David tore ahead, clear of the opposing team. Just as the shirts rammed him, Grif socked the ball back to David. He trapped it and dribbled the ball toward the opposing goal. Ralph hunched down, a hunted look on his wide face.

The shirts raced for David. He dodged, somehow keeping the ball under control.

. . . David Borelli . . . wadball . . . SOCCER CHAMPION OF THE WORLD . . .

"Pass it to me!" Rags howled.

David laughed and butted the ball into the air. A shirt player dived for it. David trapped it with the side of his foot.

"Pass it, you turd!" Rags bellowed. He was right in front of the goal.

With a last twist of his foot, David shot the ball at Rags. It hit him in the stomach, but Rags got it down. Ralph dived just as Rags whammed the ball into the net.

"Yes!" Rags shook his fists in the air.

Like a beached whale, Ralph lay on his back and groaned. Laughing, David retrieved the ball. The other guys were staring at him.

Mr. McLeod cleared his throat. "Okay, boys, now you've seen how soccer is played. Let's try it again, shall we?"

CHAPTER 14

You should've seen me," Rags bragged at dinner. Carrie's eyes widened with admiration. "I got all the goals for our team."

"Oh, wow. Do I look impressed? Is anybody going to eat that piece of meatloaf?" Betty Joseph reached her fork across the table.

Mrs. Kagan blocked her with her own fork. "You had enough. Mr. Kagan might fancy it."

David glanced toward Mr. Kagan. As always, he had already eaten, but his wheelchair was pulled up to the table. His eyes shifted around. David wondered if he had any idea what was going on around him.

"Did David play, too?" Carrie asked.

"Yeah," Rags said. "I got him on the team. He's got potential. Our first game's tomorrow night."

"What?" David put down his fork. "Why didn't you tell me?"

Rags grinned and took a long drink of water. "'Cause I wanted to break it to ya gently."

"I ain't servin' meals at all hours, so if you miss dinner, you go hungry," Mrs. Kagan warned.

"Aw, Ma," Rags protested. "Aren't you gonna pack a picnic lunch an' come cheer us on?"

"When the moon turns blue," Betty grumbled. "Carrie, d'you want your potato?"

Carrie covered it protectively. "Can I come, Rags?"

Her brother grinned. "Sure."

David was loading the dishes into the dishwasher when Scott showed up.

"Your dad's lawyer's been making some pretty interesting moves," he told David. He sipped at the coffee Mrs. Kagan had poured him. "He's submitted a bunch of motions that got the judge to put the dependency hearing off until after your dad's trial. I wouldn't have thought that he had the imagination."

"My dad does." David dropped another plate into the rack.

Scott smiled. "I guess." He hesitated. "Look, David, I know we don't have a real comfortable relationship, but I'm on your side."

David dumped the scraps into the garbage and put the plate into the dishwasher, then turned to face Scott. He felt the same as he did the night the cops broke in. As if he were groping for a knife to defend himself.

"My dad is the only family I have," he said. "You want the court to say we don't belong to each other anymore. You aren't on my side."

Scott put down the cup. "I'm trying to do what's best for you. From what I can tell, your father's always been a wild card. I don't think you're doing yourself a favor by thinking he'll rescue you."

"My family sticks together!" David yelled.

"You can't be together if your dad's in prison," Scott said gently. "You need to face facts."

David walked out.

That evening David lay on his bed, whacking a wadball between his hands, trying not to think about what Scott had said. But he couldn't help it. It was just two months until his dad's trial, and even though the lawyer was making fancy moves, it had been two weeks since he'd talked to his dad. It was just like having no family at all.

Impulsively, David took out his mom's diary and flipped through the pages.

He read about shopping for a dress for a big party, a friend whose husband had left her, doing volunteer work at the Red Cross, a fight she had with his dad . . .

"Please, Mom, help me out," David whispered. And then, as if of its own accord, the diary fell open near the end.

Treatments aren't helping. Tony can't stand seeing me sick, so he's not around much. I miss him, but I have David. My little man is the one who's looking after me now. I'm so proud of him. Guess he's grown up ahead of his time. What will happen to him? Thank God for Mrs. Rizutto. I know she'll do whatever she can for him.

I finally broke down and called Dad. Fourteen years and nothing's changed. He thought Tony'd talked me into calling to ask for money. I couldn't tell Dad that my trouble isn't money. Probably just as well. But I wish we could have mended things between us. Now it's too late.

David reread the last paragraph. Then he read it again. She said she'd *called Dad!* David chewed his lip. She must've meant David's dad—her own father had been dead for years. Hadn't he?

David closed the book, breathing hard. Think, he commanded himself. Had Mom said her dad was dead? She'd described her mother's funeral. And she'd told David about the pony her father had bought for her when she was young. But had she ever actually said her father was dead?

David's eyes strayed to the photo of Mom and her pony. A man's hand held the bridle, but he'd been cut out of the picture. Was that his grandfather? Was he still alive after all?

What had happened that was so awful that his mom had never talked about her father? His dad would know. And maybe Mrs. Rizutto. But it must have been really terrible for his mom to act as if her own father were dead.

He must be horrible, David decided, if after fourteen years he thought his daughter only wanted money. David gritted his teeth. She was dying and he never gave her a chance to tell him. And what about afterward? David hadn't met any grandfather at the funeral. There sure hadn't been any sign of him since then. He might as well be dead, for all David cared.

He switched off the light and settled back against the pillows. "Hey, Rags?"

"Yeah?" The reply was muffled by the heap of blankets.

"Do you have any grandparents?"

His roommate's head emerged. "I got a grandmother. Me and Carrie lived with her for a while."

"What happened?"

"She fell down and broke her hip. She's in a nursing home."

"Do you ever see her?"

Rags shook his head. "No. She doesn't remember stuff anymore. Like Carrie and me."

The two boys lay quietly in the dark.

"You know," Rags said, "sometimes I wonder what I did that was so bad."

"Yeah," David said. "I do, too."

"Hey, Borelli." Sean pushed him against the locker. The handle dug into David's back. "You got Ryan kicked off the team. I don't like that."

David glared back. "Ryan walked."

Sean straight-armed him in the chest. David's head slammed against the metal. "You're dead, Borelli."

He sauntered down the hall. David glared after him, rubbing the back of his head. With a yank he opened the locker, tossed in his books, and took out the soccer equipment McLeod had found for him.

A few minutes later he'd suited up with the other guys.

"Hustle! Hustle!" McLeod shouted.

David smiled as he adjusted his shin guards. It was just the way he'd imagined.

. . . *David Borelli, world champion soccer player* . . .

He trotted out and waved to Miss Bradley and Carrie, who were sitting on the grass by the edge of the field. McLeod had the boys run some easy drills to warm up. David joined the figure-eight pattern of ball passing.

In the parking lot, a yellow school bus pulled up and a bunch of boys began unloading.

Grif turned to watch. Ralph Kopowski kicked the ball out of the circle. The Shockers stopped in confusion.

"Guys, this isn't the way to scare the other team," McLeod told them.

"We're just setting 'em up." Rags kicked the ball. It spun toward Grif, who missed it by a mile.

"Who're we playing?" David asked.

The boys from the bus were trotting over to the field. They were in full uniform—yellow satin soccer shirts with red letters and matching red shorts. A couple of players passed a soccer ball back and forth between them.

"The Belmont Bulls," McLeod told him.

"Nice," Rags said. "If I transfer, can I get a fancy uniform, too, Coach, huh, Coach?"

"They'll play like losers," Grif jeered.

David watched the approaching boys. Their uniforms were as expensive as the Lakethorn Academy's. The Academy usually won their private-school championship.

"They've got a good team," McLeod told them.

"But we got a better one. Right, Davey boy?" Rags elbowed David.

"Yeah, right."

"Yeah!" Grif yelled. "Let's nail those suckers!"

For the first lineup, McLeod left David, Rags, and Grif on the sidelines.

"What's the matter with him? Doesn't he want to win?" Rags kicked the dirt.

"Saving the best for last," David retorted.

The other team was good. Within the first five minutes they'd scored two goals. Two of their forwards were so fast they ran around Ralph as if he weren't there. Ralph's face grew redder and redder.

"Uh-oh," Grif said. "Rabid Ralph's losin' it."

Just then the Bulls center midfielder jostled Ralph.

"Get outta my face!" Ralph roared. He tackled the Bulls player, sending him crashing into another Bull. All three piled onto the ground.

The Bulls' players rushed Ralph.

"Fight! Fight!" Grif yelled. His laugh brayed across the field.

The Shockers started slugging anyone in a yellow-and-red uniform. Shouting, McLeod ran toward the fight.

Rags laughed and jumped onto the bench to watch. "Davey boy, it doesn't get any better than this!"

"We'll lose!" David yelled. "We have to break it up, or we'll forfeit the game."

"So who cares?"

"I care!" David ran toward the knot of players. He grabbed one of his teammates by the shirt and hauled him backward. The boy slammed his fist into the side of David's head. David punched him back. He was so angry he didn't care whom he grabbed.

Somebody yanked him back.

"Davey boy, you're gonna get yourself killed," Rags told him. He let go and pulled a couple of Bulls off Ralph. "Fight's over!"

When they didn't seem ready to stop, Rags slammed them to the ground and bellowed a string of curses. The fighting stopped abruptly.

The two coaches glared at their teams.

"Everything's under control, sir," Rags reported to McLeod. Then he turned to the Bulls coach. "Sir, you might wanna tell your players not to shove Rabid Ralph. He's been under a lotta stress."

All eyes turned to Ralph. He dropped open his mouth, panted loudly, and let spit dribble off his tongue onto his chin.

It was so gross that David started to laugh.

"I thought we were playing a team, not a bunch of animals," one of the Bulls said.

Ralph let loose a series of grunts and squeals.

"Knock it off, Kopowski," McLeod snapped.

"Let's get on with this game," the referee ordered.

"He tackled my players!" the Bulls coach argued.

"They fouled mine!" McLeod retorted.

"Get your lineups in place!" the ref bellowed.

The two players Ralph had tackled limped off the field. This time McLeod put Rags, David, and Grif in the forward lineup and Ralph on defense. Ralph edged up between the midfielders, drooling and groaning loudly.

"You guys suck," the player opposite David sneered.

"Eat my dirt," David snapped back.

Rags kicked the ball. It sailed into the air toward the opposite goal. The Shockers raced for it.

David got there first. A Bulls defender dribbled the ball up the field, looking for an opening to pass. David kicked the ball out from under his opponent's feet. Grif intercepted the shot, then lost it to another Bull.

"Pass it to me!" Rags yelled.

Grif lunged for the ball. Ralph charged over and roared in the Bulls player's face. The boy stopped cold.

"Didn't touch 'im!" Ralph yelled to the ref.

Rags kicked the ball in the wrong direction. One of the Shockers whammed it back up the field. David got it under his foot and scanned the field, then dribbled toward the goal.

"Davey! To me!" Rags shouted.

David looked back, but Rags wasn't in position. Rapidly he dribbled the ball toward the opposing net. The goalie ran out to meet him.

The crowd cheered, wave after wave. David pulled back and kicked. The ball soared up, over the goalie, then dropped into the net.

His teammates howled. Rags thumped him on the back.

David just stood there and looked at the ball. His goal. His first real goal. He wished his dad could have seen it.

He raised his fists. The crowd cheered for David Borelli—soccer champion of North Central!!!

CHAPTER

15

The North Central Shockers won 4-3. Rabid Ralph got thrown out in the second quarter for injuring a player. By then the Bulls were so scared of Ralph's tackles and Rags' roars that they backed off and let the Shockers run off with the ball.

"I told you they'd play like losers," Grif said, laughing in the locker room.

McLeod glowered at them. "If you guys ever pull those stunts again, I'm going to shut down the team."

"But we won!" Rags said. "Mr. McLeod, we won for the first time ever!"

The boys started cheering.

Crash! Mr. McLeod's fist smashed against the locker. The boys quieted down fast.

"Winning is not what this team is about," he shouted. "Winning is not important!"

"Yes, it is," David said.

McLeod's eyes fastened on him. "So you want to win, no matter what?"

"I want to win," he said.

"Yeah!" Rags' fist shot into the air. The boys cheered.

McLeod slammed the locker again. "There's nothing wrong with winning—the right way!"

"But . . .," Rags started.

"I mean it," the coach told them. "No fouls on the other players. No dirty moves. Only good playing. And good teamwork. Practice tomorrow after school."

He strode out of the locker room.

"You told him, Borelli," Ralph giggled. "We're gonna mop 'em up. Enemies of the Shockers beware!"

David yanked off his T-shirt. No matter what McLeod said, he wanted to win. Everywhere.

"I don't know why you ain't wolfing this down." Mrs. Kagan cut another piece of steak and guided Mr. Kagan's fork to the meat. "It's nice and tender."

As he unloaded the dishwasher, David watched out of the corner of his eye. Mr. Kagan put the fork to his mouth and chewed. His eyes wandered, blank as always.

"Where's Helen?" he said suddenly.

"Right here," Mrs. Kagan soothed. "How about a nice bit of potato?"

David finished unloading and went up to his room. He flopped back on his bed and grinned, remembering the solid thump when he kicked the ball that afternoon. The Shockers were so bad they actually needed him. None of the teams at Lakethorn ever had.

Abruptly, he sat up and took a sheet of paper and a pen

from his notebook. Before he could chicken out he started writing.

Dear Dad:
　　How are you? I'm fine. Today our soccer team won its first game ever. I scored a goal and my friend Rags—Johnny Ragsdale—scored three. It was great.
　　Scott told me your lawyer got the dependency hearing put off. Maybe everything will work out. I hope so.
　　In the meantime, I'm getting on with my life, like you said. I'm going to write to you every week. I hope you write back, but if you don't, I'm going to write to you anyway.

Your son,
David

David read it over, folded the page, and put it into an envelope. His dad was fighting for him, wasn't he? He wouldn't worry about his dad writing back.

What else? His grades must be in the basement by now. David wondered if it was too late in the year to pull them up. What if he flunked?

No way. He was going to win, not fail. Tomorrow he'd talk to his teachers. After all, Sean was the stupidest rat-faced pig David had ever met. The school hadn't flunked him. And what about Rags?

His roommate came in, humming and fiddling with the telephoto lens Mr. McLeod had loaned him.

"Rags, what kind of marks does Sean get?"

"Who cares?"

"I care. How come he hasn't flunked out?"

"He cheats." Rags took the camera from his dresser and began loading a roll of film.

"What about you? Do you cheat?" David blurted out.

Rags' face reddened, but he grinned as if it were a big joke. "Davey boy, the greatest don't need to cheat."

He pulled on his earphones and cranked up the volume. David could've kicked himself. How could Rags cheat on a test he couldn't even read?

The next morning David was up, dressed, and gone before Rags had even rolled out of bed.

He dropped the letter to his dad into the mailbox on the corner, then headed to the Mini-Mart. The owner eyed him sourly while David picked out a package of baseball cards.

Rags liked sports. The cards were small—only a few words on each. It'd be a start on Rags learning to read.

Now he had to look after himself.

Mrs. Petrov, the math teacher, hugged him, offered to stay after school if he needed help, and piled a stack of assignments into his arms. David thanked her in his best Lakethorn voice.

Miss Kidd peered over her glasses, snapped out a lecture, and loaded him up with enough makeup work to get an A if he turned it in within two weeks. The Spanish and science teachers did the same.

Mr. Kilmer was last. David shifted his books as he walked into the class. His arms ached from the weight. Mr. Kilmer didn't look up from his desk.

"Excuse me, sir?"

The teacher ignored him.

"Mr. Kilmer?"

"Classes don't begin for another sixteen minutes."

"I know that, sir. But I need some extra help."

The teacher finally raised his eyes. He didn't smile or even look interested.

David felt his face heating up. "I was . . . um . . . wondering if I could do some makeup work?"

Mr. Kilmer continued to look at him as though he were a bug.

"Could I do some . . . uh . . . extra assignments . . . to pull up my grades?"

The seconds ticked away. The first bell rang.

"No, I don't think so. You had the same chances as the other students. Why should I give you special consideration?"

The kids began coming in. David walked out.

As he pitched his assignments into his locker, David imagined whacking a wadball into Kilmer's big mouth. Maybe he could still pull off a C.

"Hey, Davey boy!" Rags threaded his way through the crowd of students. "You got some cute little lady hidden around here? Or is this dump so great you gotta rush over early?"

"Rags, I got something for you." David took the package of cards from his pocket.

Rags took the package and turned it over with interest, then split it open. "Baseball cards. Cool." Rags grinned. "But, Davey boy, you know my sport is soccer."

"Yeah, I know," David said in a rush, "but I figured I could teach you the words on the cards. You know . . . so you could read them."

Rags' smile froze.

"You're gonna teach Rags the *words*?" David hadn't heard Sean come up in the crowd. The bully's small eyes narrowed.

Rags dropped the cards and walked away.

"Rags!" David started after him, but Sean grabbed his shoulders and slammed him against the row of lockers. The metal vibrated against David's back. Foul breath spread over his face. He stared into the little pig eyes.

"Whaddya mean, you're gonna teach Rags the *words*?" Sean demanded.

David knew he was a dead man. It didn't matter. Not after what he'd done to Rags.

"Moskovitz," Grif interrupted, "leave the guy alone."

"Not a chance." Sean never took his tiny eyes off David.

"You mess with our best soccer player, an' Rags'll rip your heart out," Grif warned. "We won last night!"

"Talk to me, butthead." Sean jabbed an elbow into David's chest.

Go ahead! Tear my arms off, David thought. "This is none of your business," he said aloud.

"Oh, excu-u-use me!" Sean did a lousy Steve Martin imitation.

David grinned. He couldn't help it. It was so bad. "There's no excuse for you . . . *pig breath!*"

The silence in the hall was like hot steam. David tensed, knowing he was dead, knowing it would be worth it to really stand up to Sean—to everybody.

The bully grunted into action. He grabbed David's shirt and shoved him into the open locker. The coat hooks jabbed David's head. He tried to shove back. Sean guffawed and pressured the door shut.

"No!" David yelled. The door pushed tighter; David felt his lungs compressing. Was he going to die in a locker?

"There's no excuse for you!" he shouted again.

The locker door slammed against him. His lungs ached. His back was breaking. He couldn't breathe.

Then abruptly the door swung loose. David lurched out. *Wham!!*

Rags slammed Sean against the wall. The lockers vibrated like a giant dentist's drill. Sean's gang melted into the circle of watching students.

"I warned you, man." Grif folded his arms on his chest, ready to enjoy the show. "You're dead, Moskovitz."

Ralph giggled. Nobody else said anything. It was dead quiet, like the eye of a hurricane.

Sean swung. Rags caught the fist and twisted it down and behind, then jammed his forearm against Sean's throat. Rags kneed Sean once, twice in the gut. The bully's face turned a weird shade of red, and he gasped for air.

"Stupid move, Moskovitz," Rags snarled. "Davey is my roommate. We got an understanding. And my business"—he jabbed Sean again—"is my business."

"Rags! Break it up!" The crowd parted. Mr. McLeod strode through. He grabbed Rags' shoulder. "You promised me!"

Rags let go of Sean and stepped back, breathing hard. The bully sagged against the locker.

"Way to go, Rags!" Ralph cheered.

"Did I tell 'im?" Grif slapped David on the back.

"Shut up! All of you!" McLeod snapped.

"Aw, he deserved it," Grif replied. "Right, Borelli?"

"What's going on here?" Thin Lips pushed through the kids, then glared at Mr. McLeod. "You said if I gave that boy another chance, the fights would stop."

The bell rang suddenly, jarring everyone into action. The halls cleared. Only David, Rags, Sean, Mr. McLeod, and Thin Lips were left.

Sean lurched to his feet. Thin Lips looked at him as if he smelled bad. "You'd better go down to the nurse. Do you need any help?"

"No!" Sean jerked himself straight and spit at Rags. Rags sidestepped. "Yer finished, Rags. An' when yer outta here, I'm gonna waste that little turd. . . ."

"Stow it, Moskovitz," McLeod snapped. He gave Sean the coldest look David had ever seen. Sean faltered, then stumbled down the hall.

"Down to my office, Ragsdale," Thin Lips ordered.

McLeod ran his hand tiredly through his hair. "Better get to class, David."

"No, sir," David replied. "This is my fault."

"Butt out, Borelli!" Rags growled.

David shook his head and bent down to pick up the baseball cards. McLeod shrugged. They all went down to the vice principal's office.

Thin Lips took a folder from a filing cabinet and sat at his desk. He turned the pages slowly. Rags shifted from one foot to another, breathing hard. David fingered the cards in his pocket.

"Well, Ragsdale," Thin Lips finally said, "you've been suspended twice for fighting. Your academic scores are nonexistent, and the police have come here several times to question you about breaking into people's homes. Quite a remarkable picture."

"Guess I'm a remarkable person." Rags grinned, but his face had gone a funny color.

David bit his lip. Carrie'd said Rags was bad. He hadn't guessed how bad.

"Shut up, Rags," Mr. McLeod snapped. "Mr. Thelps, Johnny hasn't been in any kind of trouble for nearly six months. And Sean's fights are well known."

Thin Lips shut the folder. "Sean is not on probation from the courts. And his family is working with him."

"Let me get this straight," McLeod interrupted. "You're letting Sean off the hook because his parents are working with him?"

"He is not a ward of the state!" Thin Lips snapped. "Ragsdale, this will have to be reported to Child Protective Services."

"Who cares?" Rags folded his arms over his chest and stared out the window.

"Wait!" David interrupted. "I started the problem, then Sean started the fight. Rags saved me!"

Thin Lips regarded him for a moment. "By beating up Sean. People are responsible for their own actions."

"Yeah, that's what my old lady taught me," Rags sneered.

"Rags, stop it!" David ground out. "Sir, you don't understand. Rags can't read!"

"What?" Mr. McLeod rounded on him.

"Shut up, Borelli!" Rags yelled.

"Rags, you need help!" David shouted back. He turned to Mr. McLeod and repeated "Rags can't read."

"I told you to shut up!" Rags swung at David. It went wide.

McLeod grabbed Rags' shoulders and jerked him around. "Is this true, Rags? Is that what's been going on?"

The boy tried to twist away.

"Why didn't you tell me?" Mr. McLeod demanded. "I'm your friend!"

Rags shoved him away. "I got a lot of friends, man. And teachers, too. They ain't never done me any good!" He ran out.

Mr. McLeod swore softly.

"Go back to class, David," Thin Lips ordered.

"What about Rags?"

"Go on to class," Mr. McLeod said. "I'll catch you at soccer practice later."

David left the office, walked out the front door, and headed for the mall. No sign of Rags. When David went back to school, his friend still wasn't in class. At soccer practice McLeod met David's eyes and shook his head.

The team practiced drills. They scrimmaged. For once the boys tried to follow McLeod's directions.

"Good job, men!" McLeod told them after an hour and a half. "Same time tomorrow."

"Man, we're the best," Ralph gloated as they headed into the locker room.

"Hey, Borelli," Grif asked, "what happened to Rags?"

"I don't know."

"Well, he'd better show up for the game on Friday," Grif declared. "I wanna win. I mean, my dad even said maybe I wasn't such a total loser after all. Majorly unreal." He wandered off, shaking his head.

David got his books and headed home. He didn't run. He wasn't going to run from anyone anymore.

CHAPTER

16

The social workers had already swooped down on the Kagans' and carried Rags away.

"Assessments," explained Betty Joseph. "They always do assessments on kids like us. Like they'll make a difference." She rolled her eyes.

Mrs. Kagan slammed dishes around in the kitchen. Carrie sobbed uncontrollably in her room. Betty Joseph fled to her boyfriend's house.

The next day Mr. McLeod wasn't in school. But Sean was. As the kids crowded through the halls to change classes, he cornered David by his locker.

"You're gonna die, butthead," he gloated.

David felt a chill run over him, but he stared straight into the bully's face. "Back off," he said. "You don't scare me anymore."

Sean laughed. "I don't wanna scare you, butthead—I wanna kill you!"

"Don't bet on it," replied David. He deliberately turned his back on Sean.

It'll come now, he thought. He'll nail me from behind.

He started walking. One step . . . two . . . then five . . . then ten. A line of sweat trickled down his back and into the crack in his rear.

"Hey! Get outta my way!"

Surprised, David whipped around. Rabid Ralph and Grif had blocked Sean.

"Moskovitz, you're goin' the wrong way." Ralph laughed like a crazy person and bumped Sean with his big stomach.

"Stay away from 'im, Sean," Grif warned. "He's our teammate. An' there's a lot more guys on the team than you got in your gang—*Pig breath!*"

Grinning, they walked toward David.

"Hey, Borelli," Ralph called. "Wait up!"

For the rest of the day, Ralph and Grif, and sometimes their other teammates, laughed and joked on either side of David as they walked the halls. Then some of the girls came along, too. It was great, except that Rags never showed up.

David cut out before his last class and headed home. The social worker's car pulled away from the curb in front of the Kagans' just as he rounded the corner.

Breathing hard, David ran down the sidewalk and tore into the house. He raced up the stairs just as Rags came out of the bathroom.

"Rags!" David cried. "Are you okay?"

His roommate's eyes flamed; then he shouldered by. David followed him into the bedroom.

"Rags," he pleaded. "Somebody had to know—so they could help you!"

Rags pulled on his earphones and cranked up the volume. Furious, David tore them off.

"Talk to me!" he yelled.

For a second Rags looked as if he'd pound David, but then he turned his back. "I don't know you, Borelli!"

From then on it was as if Rags became somebody else. Zombieman, David thought.

At school Rags walked around by himself. He didn't talk to anyone he didn't have to, except Carrie. Most nights he stayed after school until late.

When the Shockers played against other schools, Rags never bellowed for David to pass the ball. David kicked it to him anyhow.

Rags played his position. He listened to McLeod. His kicks weren't wide anymore. The rest of the Shockers followed his lead. With David setting up the ball and Grif flanking them, they scored goal after goal.

Mr. McLeod cheered from the sidelines. So did Carrie and Miss Bradley. And all the other kids. The whole student body turned out for the Shockers games. For the first time, North Central students were winners.

David detailed the wins to his dad in a weekly letter. And then one afternoon there was a letter in a plain white envelope waiting.

Dear David:

    I have your stack of letters in front of me. You know now they can't take Anthony Borelli's son without a fight! The dependency lawyer did what I told him, so I'm making CPS and the courts work for what they want.

I've been meeting with the court-appointed defense lawyer. He's an idiot. With him handling my trial, the legal system will chew me up into little pieces—and the press will lap it up!

I won't write again—not because I don't care about you—but because I don't want to drag you down with me.

Love, Dad

David read the letter about six times. He couldn't believe it! It was just like his dad. If Anthony Borelli couldn't be the big-time winner, then he'd be the self-sacrificing hero. And David would still be left behind.

He threw the letter into the trash and went outside. He started running, faster and faster. His feet pounded the pavement. His breath came in gasps. The sweat streaked down his forehead and back. Then he settled into a steady, mile-eating lope.

Block after block he traveled—past small shops, Old Belmont mansions on the lake, up into the expensive suburbs—until the ivy-covered walls of his old school came into view.

David bought himself a big bottle of pop and sat drinking it on the curb across from the Lakethorn Academy. He pushed his long hair out of his eyes, then sauntered across the street to the shadow of the trees that lined the soccer field. The school team was practicing.

With an experienced eye, he assessed their playing. The offense was strong, but their defense kept moving out of position. And not one of them roared or belly-danced like Rabid Ralph. David grinned and took another swig of pop. The Lakethorn Eagles just didn't have any class.

He recognized all the boys, but they seemed like strangers. David shook his head in mild surprise. He didn't belong here anymore.

At the convenience store he dropped a quarter into the pay phone and dialed Mrs. Rizutto's number.

She answered on the first ring, as if she'd been standing there waiting.

"Hello?"

"Hi, Mrs. Rizutto."

"David! You are all right? Do you need anything?"

"No. I'm fine. I would've called before, but I've been busy with soccer practice and trying to pull good grades in my classes."

"Your mama would be proud of you." Pause. "Do you hear from your papa?"

"Yeah. I had a letter from him today. He said he's got a bad lawyer, and I guess he's looking at a long jail term."

She sighed. "He's not good enough for you or your mama. But you know this."

"He's still my dad. Mrs. Rizutto, where does my grandfather live?"

There was silence on the other end.

"Mrs. Rizutto?"

"I promised your mama not to tell you about him."

David's stomach lurched. He did have a grandfather! "But I already know. You have to tell me! What did he do? Is he a criminal or something?"

"Mr. Gilman?" Mrs. Rizutto's voice sounded aghast. "No! No! . . . David, I think we should meet to talk about this. Are you at your foster home?"

"No. I'm near my old school."

"You wait there. I get my Joe to drive me, then we will talk."

Less than twenty minutes later David faced Mrs. Rizutto across a table at a McDonald's. She'd sent her son, Joe, to the counter for coffee and hamburgers.

"Tell me what happened," David said.

Mrs. Rizutto tapped her fingers on the table. "I told your mama she was wrong to not tell you, but she is stubborn."

David nodded. "So am I."

Mrs. Rizutto smiled at him. "That I know. . . . Your mama fell in love with your papa when she was very young. Only eighteen. Her father had always told her what she must do and who she must be friends with, and then she would not listen anymore. He was very angry."

"Did he throw her out?"

Mrs. Rizutto looked surprised. "No. He would never do that."

"I don't understand," David said impatiently. "What happened?"

"Your mama and papa sneaked away and got married. He was twelve years older than she was, and Mr. Gilman—and me also—thought he only wanted the money."

"Money?"

"Yes. Mr. Gilman is very rich."

David felt his head spinning. He'd gotten hazed because he couldn't afford a lousy T-shirt and now he finds out he has a rich grandfather.

"But," Mrs. Rizutto went on, "he did not want to lose his daughter, so he gave your papa a very good job in his company."

"So what happened?"

Mrs. Rizutto sighed. "It was not enough. Your papa wanted the big cars and a boat and a big house all at once. His salary wasn't enough. So he made invoices that were not real and took the money from the company."

David took a deep breath. "And Mom sided with Dad."

Mrs. Rizutto nodded sadly. "She is loyal always. Mr. Gilman thought he could make her end this bad marriage, so he had your papa arrested."

"Did he go to jail?"

"No. Your mama used the money she'd inherited from her mother to pay for a very smart lawyer. Your papa was set free. But your mama and Mr. Gilman had a terrible fight and did not speak again. She believed that her husband was innocent but that her papa had tried to make him look guilty. She said her papa had betrayed her."

David rubbed his hands through his hair. Joe came back carrying a tray loaded with food, but David sprang up and pushed past him.

"David!" Mrs. Rizutto called.

He kept going.

CHAPTER

17

David pulled on his team T-shirt, adjusted his shin pads, and tightened the knots in his soccer shoes.

"Man, we're gonna waste 'em," Ralph gloated as he pulled his own extra large T-shirt over his stomach. "Isn't that right, Rags?"

"Yeah, sure," Rags replied, and headed out to the field.

"That guy's real down these days," Grif commented. "Don't he realize we're about to win the city championship?"

"Maybe I should give him a belly bounce!" Ralph grinned and rotated his stomach. "That'd make him happy . . . or else!"

"*Yeah!*"

"*Do it! Do it!*" his teammates cheered.

"Leave him alone," David snapped.

The guys turned to him in surprise. David thought fast.

"Look, this is our big game. Do you think it's smart to belly bounce our best scorer?"

"Dumb . . . but fun!" Ralph erupted into a series of barks and woofs.

Grif grinned. "Down, boy! We'll get you somebody else, Ralphie. Maybe the other team's goalie."

Ralph panted happily.

McLeod came in. His eyes were twinkling as he laid a hand on Ralph's shoulder. "Try to think human."

"But, Coach, Rabid Ralph is our secret weapon!" Grif declared.

"Not when we have your foot, Albert."

The boys looked at each other in amazement.

"Right." Grif leaned to whisper into David's ear. "Coach's been drinking happy juice."

"Okay, now, hustle up, men! Nearly game time!"

As the boys trotted onto the field the crowd around the sidelines cheered and hooted. The Shockers shook their fists in the air and shouted, "Yay Shockers! The best! The best! The *best!*"

Ralph did his belly dance in the center of the field. The crowd went wild.

The Interlake Rams huddled together and stared at the madmen opposite them, while the coaches conferred with the referee. McLeod called out the lineup. David, Rags, and Grif were on the bench.

"Coach," Grif protested. "You gotta play us now! Y'know! Hit 'em hard, so we get the edge."

"Ralph gave us enough of an edge already," McLeod retorted.

David grinned and risked a look at Rags. For once he was grinning, too.

The Rams scored a goal within the first three minutes of play. Ralph roared, but the opposing team's player only backed away about ten feet.

"Tough team," Grif commented.

"Not too tough for us," said David.

Rags grunted.

"Okay, boys," McLeod said, "first break, I'm sending you in."

"We're ready!"

"Anytime!"

Just then Rabid Ralph lost it. Grabbing the ball with both hands, he steamrollered up the field. All the players scattered. David and his teammates jumped to their feet.

"He's out of his mind!" David yelled.

"Ralph! Ralph! Ralph!" The North Central fans cheered.

"I'll kill him!" McLeod growled.

Ralph thrust aside the opposing team's players and bounced the ball off the goalie's head.

"That stupid . . . !" McLeod groaned.

Ralph hula danced across the field. The crowd went wild. The referee threw him out of the game and awarded the Rams a free kick.

"Hey, we've lost before," Rags told McLeod.

"Not this time!" David snapped.

By the time McLeod sent their string onto the field the Rams were out for blood. David took elbow jabs, shin kicks, and a body slam. The referee had gone blind. No fouls were called.

"What're we gonna do?" Grif demanded at halftime.

"We'll take 'em out, one by one," a sweeper said.

"No way," McLeod ordered. "We play hard—but we

play fair! If I catch any of you—" he stopped and stared at each of them in turn—"even trying to foul another player, I'll forfeit the game."

"Coach," Grif said in alarm, "you can't do that!"

"Sure, he can," Rags sneered. "At North Central we might look like idiots, but we do it right."

"Rags, don't screw this up. You guys have been winning because for the first time in your lives you've been playing as a team." McLeod put his hand on the boy's shoulder.

"Leave me alone! I don't need a team!" Rags twisted away and headed out to the field.

The coach shook his head in exasperation. "Okay, guys! Let's go."

The whistle blew for the game to start again. From then on the ball belonged to the Rams. The Shockers couldn't do anything right. Rags kicked as if his feet had been smeared with Krazy Glue. Grif missed every pass. The ball went nowhere.

During an offside Rags finally edged over to David. "Give it up, Borelli," he sneered. "We're all losers."

David froze. The ball whizzed by him and he didn't move. A few guys in the crowd hooted. Furious, David yanked Rags around.

"I'm a winner!" he shouted.

"Yeah, sure," Rags snarled.

McLeod bellowed from the sidelines. The game raced on around them.

"Yeah! And don't you forget it!" David told him.

The ball spun their way. David captured it and dribbled down the field. Rags paced him.

"Go, Shockers! Go!" the crowd yelled.

The Rams defense pounded toward them. David looked

for a clear shot. Nothing. Rags loped toward the goal.

David kicked, sure and hard. Rags controlled the ball smoothly and whammed it into the net.

The crowd screamed. The Shockers pranced, fists raised. Rags kicked the dirt.

Rags and David scored three more goals. David gasped for air—he'd never played so hard. One more goal. Just one.

The ball winged up from their defense. David trapped it and shot it to Rags. Rags dribbled the ball back and forth, wasting time. At the last minute he passed it to Grif.

Surprised, Grif nearly missed it. But he got his foot around the ball, loped toward the goal, and thumped it into the net.

Five to four.

Shockers. City champions!

With the rest of his team, David shouted and yelled. Rags picked up the ball and silently tossed it from hand to hand. Ralph climbed to the top of the stands and danced.

A smartly tailored woman, whom David guessed was a city council member, walked onto the field. A man ran beside her, stringing a microphone onto the playing field, while yet another walked behind carrying a plaque and a huge trophy.

Grinning, Mr. McLeod and the team stood waiting on the field.

"Incredible game," the woman said.

"Great bunch of boys," McLeod replied.

The city council member took the microphone and made a short speech to the cheering crowd. The boys rolled their eyes.

". . . and it is my pleasure to present the Roberts Trophy for Junior Interschool Soccer to the North Central Shockers!" The crowd screamed. "Could your coach and team captain come forward to accept it, please."

The boys eyed each other in confusion. David pushed Rags forward. "Here's our captain, Johnny Ragsdale!" he said loudly.

The team shouted approval.

"Your school has the honor of displaying this trophy for the next year," the councilwoman said, presenting it to Mr. McLeod. Her assistant handed her a large plaque, which she held up and then handed to Rags. "The plaque is the school's to keep." She held the microphone up to Rags. "How about reading the inscription?"

David froze. Rags' eyes darted to Mr. McLeod.

"Go ahead, Rags," Mr. McLeod said. "Give it a shot."

Rags licked his lips and looked down at the plaque. A long moment passed. David could feel the sweat building on his forehead. Why didn't McLeod do something?

Rags' eyes went to the coach's again. McLeod nodded encouragement.

Speaking slowly, Rags read out, "This trophy is awarded to the All-City Junior Champion Soccer Team." He held up the plaque. *"North Central Shockers! We're the winners!"*

The crowd cheered, wave after wave of sound. The Shockers howled and stamped their feet. Above them Ralph belly danced. Rags held the plaque aloft.

"Way to go, Rags," David shouted over the din.

McLeod put one hand on Rags' shoulder and lifted the big trophy high with the other.

Afterward Mr. McLeod took the team out for a victory pizza. Carrie and Miss Bradley came, too.

"Hey, Davey boy!" Rags slid onto the bench beside David. "I got some soccer cards."

"Yeah?"

"Yeah. Mr. McLeod made me." He stared at the menu on the board. "I've been ready to kill you."

David nodded. "I know."

Rags turned and looked at him for the first time. He shrugged. "I owe you, man."

David grinned and punched Rags on the arm. Laughing, Rags shoved him back.

"Settle down, guys," McLeod ordered.

The pizzas came, and the boys started grabbing and gulping. It was not a pretty sight.

Carrie'd wiggled onto the bench beside David. She tugged his shirt. "Miss Bradley has a ring," she whispered.

"So what?" David grabbed for another slice. Pepperoni and sausage this time.

Carrie tugged his shirt again. "She's going to marry Mr. McLeod!"

The whole team heard. Ralph and Grif started hooting.

"Tsk, tsk," Rags said.

Miss Bradley blushed furiously, and even Mr. McLeod turned a little red.

Then the jokes started. David laughed so hard he thought he was going to be sick. It was the best night he'd had in as long as he could remember.

CHAPTER

18

They were late getting home. Yawning, laughing, and stomping, David and Rags finally made it to bed. Within moments Rags' breathing settled into a heavy pattern of sleep. David lay wide awake, arms folded behind his head. It had been easy to forget about the rest of his life during the soccer game.

Impulsively, David got out of bed and headed downstairs for a glass of milk. To his surprise Mrs. Kagan was standing by the stove waiting for a kettle to boil. The teapot stood ready.

"Mr. Kagan's having one of his bad nights," she said.

David reached up for a glass. "Is he . . . is Mr. Kagan going to get better?"

Mrs. Kagan blinked suddenly. "No," she said. "He's not going to get better." She tried to smile, but her mouth quivered and she bit her lip.

The kettle started to boil and she busied herself making

the tea. David poured his milk, then stood there holding the glass, watching her.

"What will you do?"

"What? Oh, sell the house, I guess. No need for this big place just for me."

"You won't be fostering anymore, then?"

"I'm getting old, David. And worn out." She poured her mug of tea. "And what are you doing up this time of night? Don't be expecting me to get you out of bed in the morning."

"I won't, Ma."

She patted his shoulder. "Things change, David. If they didn't, nothing could ever get better."

"Or worse."

"True enough. But some of it's choice." She picked up her tea. "I've got to get back to Mr. Kagan, and you better get to bed."

She went out of the kitchen. David held the glass of milk and stared at the wall. The idea of a new foster home made him sick. In his gut he knew his dad was guilty and was going to jail. Scott was right. No matter what fast moves his dad had pulled, the dependency hearing was a done deal.

David scowled. And what would that do to him? Would he become one of the hunch-shouldered losers? No way! Rags' life had been a walking disaster, but he'd kept fighting. And David wasn't going to shrug off his own life either.

He dumped the milk down the sink and went back upstairs. Taking a notebook and pen with him, David headed into the bathroom. The only place to be in the middle of the night.

He sat on the toilet, ripped out a sheet of paper, and

started writing. The words poured out as though he'd worked them out a long time ago.

Dear Dad,

You've told me a couple of times to get on with my life. I have. My team won the city soccer championship today and next week we go on to the regional finals. I'm getting A's in almost all of my classes (not social studies—the teacher's a real jerk).

Anyway, I did what you asked, and I'll keep doing it because I like being a winner. But I still want a father, even if I won't get to live with you again.

I want you to write to me every week, just like I write to you. I want you to talk to me, because no matter what the courts say, we're all the family we've got.

Your son,
David

David read the letter over again, then folded it, ready to go in an envelope. He paused. His mom had died before she could fix things with her dad. The old man had been horrible to her, thinking the only thing that mattered was money. But she hadn't been very smart to believe Tony Borelli was innocent. In the end, though, his mom had tried to call her father.

David went back to his bedroom and got out the diary. Rags snored peacefully under his heap of blankets. By the moonlight filtering through the window, David found the diary entry and tore it out. Then he went back to the bathroom.

Taking a fresh sheet from the notebook, David carefully

addressed the top as if it were a business letter. Then he wrote, "Dear Grandfather." He stopped. Should it be Mr. Gilman?

David ground his teeth, balled the sheet up, and with a neat kick sent it flying to the corner of the bathtub.

He started again . . . and again . . .

The pile of wadballs was six deep. David tore out another sheet and decided that this time he'd just write it, no matter how stupid it sounded.

Dear Grandfather,

I don't know if you know who I am. I'm your grandson, David. My mother never told me about you. I found out by reading her diary after she died.

Mom wanted to fix things with you but couldn't do it. I'm sending you the page from her diary. Even though it's been a long time, I guess you know her writing.

Mom always said, "If a family isn't loyal, there's no family." I don't know if she was right, but I'm trying to be loyal to her. It's part of being a winner.

David hesitated. Had his grandfather seen the newspaper stories about his father? Biting his lip, David kept writing.

You may have seen some newspaper stories about my father. He has a good lawyer. I am living with a nice family and I'm fine.

Yours truly
David Borelli (your grandson)
P.S. I don't need any money.

David sat back and yawned. It was done. He'd call Mrs.

Rizutto in the morning and get his grandfather's address. He went to bed, knowing he'd done everything he could think of to make the changes good ones.

David glanced at the scoreboard. Four all. About three minutes left in regulation time. The Flames had already won two games in the playoffs to the Shockers' one. If they scored now, they took the regional championship.

Grif threw in. Rags brought it down and socked it toward the Flames goal. David and Grif raced for the ball. Two of the Flames defenders charged them. David leaped sideways and hurtled toward the ball.

Rags was pounding up the center of the field. David kicked. The goalie threw himself on the ball, then in a smooth motion jumped up and kicked it downfield. Rags fell back and intercepted. The Flames players converged on him.

"Pass it to me!" David yelled.

Rags hesitated.

"Eat my dirt!" Rags yelled at the Flames.

"Rags!" McLeod bellowed from the sidelines. *"Teamwork!"*

Once again Rags hesitated. Then with a string of curses, he shot the ball to David. David got it down and dribbled toward the goal. The Flames players veered and started toward him. Rags broke free and tore up the field.

David caught his breath. The goalie was ready for him. Last chance.

"To me!" Rags yelled.

David glanced over. Rags was in position. Just as the Flames reached him, David sent the ball sideways, over their heads. Rags leaped up, knocked it down, and booted it into the goal.

The whistle blew.

"Yes!" The Shockers howled and high-fived. They yelled and thumped each other on the back. Then they grabbed McLeod and tried to carry him around. When they couldn't lift him, the boys dumped their water bottles all over him.

"Good game . . . good game . . . good game . . ." David slapped the hands of his opponents.

By the bench, Miss Bradley was laughing and helping Mr. McLeod wring water from his sweatshirt.

A gray-haired man in a business suit weaved through the crowd and touched McLeod's arm. His eyes swept over the boys churning around the field. "Mr. McLeod? I'm looking for a boy on your team. David Borelli?"

McLeod glanced at him, distracted. "What . . . yeah, sure . . . hey, David!"

David detached himself from Rags' headlock, laughingly threw the soccer ball at him, and trotted over to Mr. McLeod. "Yeah, Coach?"

"This gentleman wants to talk to you." He pulled his wet sweatshirt back over his head.

David stood stock-still, staring at the old gentleman. He in turn gazed searchingly at David.

Mr. McLeod stepped closer. "I don't think we've met, Mr. . . .?"

The man pulled his eyes from David. "Gilman. Robert Gilman. I'm David's grandfather."

David and his grandfather eyed each other over the white linen of the restaurant table. In the distance elegant sailboats skimmed over the lake. For several minutes they'd busied themselves with the menu, but the waiter had taken their order.

"Excellent game," his grandfather said finally.

"Thanks."

"Just one more win for the regional trophy?"

"That's right." David nodded.

"My college football team won its division. That was the best time of my life." He pleated his napkin, a series of long sharp folds. "When your mother left was the worst. Your letter . . ." He fumbled inside his jacket pocket and produced David's letter. "Your letter was a great joy to me."

David's face heated up. "You didn't come to her funeral."

"Yes, I did. But I stayed out of sight. I didn't know how your father would react to me. And I expected you had been taught to hate me."

David shook his head. "No. I didn't even know you were alive."

"As you can see, I am."

The waiter brought their lunches. David's was a monstrous cheeseburger surrounded by frilled lettuce and carved tomatoes. His grandfather had a small steak.

"I suppose the program at your middle school is less difficult than at Lakethorn," Mr. Gilman went on.

David thought about Sean and his gang. "It's different."

"Yes. Well, enjoy your lunch."

David bit into his cheeseburger. It was juicy with ground steak and sharp cheddar cheese. He thought maybe he like fast-food ones better.

His grandfather buttered a roll, then put it down again without tasting it. "You look very much like her."

David didn't know what to say, so he took another bite.

He swiped at his chin with a linen napkin when the juices spurted out, then smiled. The teachers at Lakethorn would be appalled. They taught their charges excellent table manners. On the other hand, at North Central the guys wiped their chins with the backs of their arms and were food-fight champs.

"But I suppose you're like your father as well."

"I suppose." David eyed his grandfather across the table. What was the old man getting at?

"The state agencies have approached me about assuming guardianship for you."

David said slowly, "But I told you in my letter, I don't want anything from you."

"Indeed?" His grandfather's face grew stony. "Your father does. They're charging him for the costs of the dependency hearings."

"He knew they'd do that."

"Your father always has an angle. He offered to withdraw his appeals and recommend me for guardianship, providing I paid his legal bills. And then your letter came. I couldn't help but wonder if he suggested you contact me as well."

David carefully put the hamburger down on his plate and stood up.

"Thank you for lunch, sir. And don't worry about guardianship or Dad's legal costs. I'll tell the court I don't want anything to do with you." He walked toward the entrance.

"David!" his grandfather called. "David, wait!"

David kept going. Outside, the wind from the lake blew

smoothly, ruffling the trees of Old Belmont.

He began to run, faster and faster, feeling the solid pavement thwack beneath his feet. His breath came in gasps, not from running but from rage. With his father and his grandfather, it always came down to money.

He never wanted to see either of them again!

CHAPTER

19

The score was two all. David rubbed a fist across his face, leaving a streak of dirt. He glanced up at the scoreboard. Six minutes left in the last quarter. One more goal—just one for the regional championship.

The ref had thrown Ralph out when he tried to bulldoze the Freemont Flames goalie. The Flames were angry—and they were tough.

The ref signaled for the throw in.

"Where's Rabid Ralph when we need 'im?" Rags grunted.

David grinned. "Their right defender's nearly worn out. I'll try to bring the ball up through there."

"I'll be ready."

The Flames sweeper threw in. The Shockers defense charged. The boys fought for the ball in a tight, grunting circle. Finally a Shockers sweeper kicked the ball between the legs of the Flames center midfielder.

David intercepted the pass. The Flames tore up the

field toward him. Rags loped down the center of the field. David dribbled the ball toward the net. The Flames defense tried to trip him, but David jumped over the out-stretched feet and kept going.

The crowd cheered louder and louder.

The Shockers offense ringed David, shouldering aside the Flames players.

"*Shockers! Shockers! Shockers!*" the crowd screamed. The noise pounded in David's ears.

"Pass it, Davey boy!" Rags bellowed.

David looked for a clear shot. A Flames player, trying to get close enough to defend his goal, plowed into Rags. Rags shook him off, but the Flames defense crowded him away.

The Shockers wing hesitated. David tried to line up a shot to Grif. Couldn't do it.

"*Shockers! Shockers! Shockers!*" the crowd howled.

"Take it in!" Rags yelled.

The Flames charged. David broke clear, drew back, and kicked. The ball soared high, past the goalie—into the net.

Three to two!

The boys scuffled for the ball at midfield. Grif got it under his feet and booted it to David. He passed it to Rags. Playing for time. Two minutes. One. . . .

The referee's whistle blew. *Shockers: Regional Champions!*

Rags hoisted David up on his shoulders. The spectators stampeded down from the stands. Rabid Ralph did his belly dance at midfield.

The Shockers yelled and pounded each other on the back. A laughing official tried to call order for the presentation of the trophy, then finally gave up.

Robert Gilman jostled through the crowd. His eyes swept over the pandemonium on the field, then located the coach chatting with the officials.

Mr. Gilman strode over. "Mr. McLeod, I'm looking for David."

McLeod grinned. "Sure thing. You've got quite a player there.

Gilman nodded. "I know."

The coach waved his arm. "Hey, David!"

David thumped a team member on the back, whipped the ball at Rags, and turned to his coach.

He stopped cold, then abruptly turned on his heel and rejoined the tussle of celebrating team members.

McLeod looked appraisingly at Gilman. "David doesn't seem too thrilled to see you."

The old man stared at the crowd of boys. "No, he doesn't."

He turned and left.

From the safety of his stomping and shouting teammates, David watched his grandfather leave. Rags grabbed his jersey and hauled him to the other side of the mob. "Hey, Davey boy, who's the old guy?"

"My grandfather." David jerked free.

Another wave of cheers rang out as Ralph swung from a goalpost, dropped, and gyrated.

"Cool."

"Yeah, right."

"At least he remembers you, man. That's worth something."

The crowd surged around them. David shoved his

grandfather from his mind and whooped and roared with his friends.

Later they celebrated with pizza and shouts and laughter, until the owner of the restaurant wanted to throw them out. But when he saw their trophy he gave them dessert on the house.

"I went to North Central," he declared, and joined the team in the shouting and laughing.

When David and Rags finally got home that evening, David found a letter on the kitchen table addressed to him. The return address was the county jail.

"Love letters?" Rags demanded. He pulled a milk carton from the fridge and drank long gulps from the spout.

David shook his head. "My dad."

He turned the letter over a couple of times.

"You gonna read it? Or should I?"

David grinned. "Don't get carried away." He ripped the envelope open.

Dear David,

Great news. Your grandfather Gilman came to see me today. Somehow, you blew the old guy away. He's offered to pay my court costs and legal fees—not because I deserve it (true enough)—but because he thinks you'd like it. Something about family loyalty?

I don't know how you did it, but you've cracked the old gent. No one else, including your mother, has ever been able to do that. He'll give you whatever you want. Enjoy it, son.

Keep the letters coming.

Dad

David didn't know whether to throw up or laugh. He crumpled up the letter and threw it into the trash.

Rags took another swig of milk. "Good news or bad?"

"Beats me."

Rags dropped the empty container on top of the letter, then threw his arm around David's shoulders. "Davey boy, nothin' but good things can happen to us."

"Why's that?" David started to laugh.

Rags grinned. "Because we're the greatest!"

When they walked into school the next morning, the other students seemed to agree with Rags. David, Rags, and the other team members were smacked on the back and followed around the halls by their friends. Sean and his gang kept their distance.

The news of the North Central Shockers' victory was the first morning announcement. Students in all the classes started cheering until the roar reverberated over the crackling PA system.

David shut his eyes. It was better than all the imaginary crowds put together.

When he and Rags sauntered home that night, an ambulance was parked in front of the house.

Rags cursed. Together they ran for the front door and raced in.

Betty Joseph met them wide-eyed at the door.

"It's Mr. Kagan," she told them.

They stood there, unsure what to do until Mrs. Kagan and the two paramedics walked slowly from the back of the house.

"Just keep him quiet," one of the paramedics said. "You can bring him to his doctor if you want, but he seems stable now."

"Yes . . . thank you," Mrs. Kagan said. The paramedics left.

She stood a moment watching after them, then suddenly turned to the kids. "What're you three standin' around here for?"

"Is Mr. Kagan okay?" David asked.

Mrs. Kagan's lips quivered, but she snapped out, "Of course he's okay. Just had a little fall, that's all—and not even a sprain neither, the paramedics say."

"Great," Rags said cautiously.

"Do you want us to make you some tea?" David asked.

"Since when do you make me tea?" Mrs. Kagan demanded.

"Since you need a cup, Ma." Rags took her arm and steered her toward the kitchen. "You sit down, and Davey boy'll get the kettle boiling."

Mrs. Kagan sank down, then started to jump up again. "Mr. Kagan . . ."

"I'll go sit with him," Betty Joseph said, and disappeared into the back bedroom.

"You're all no good," Mrs. Kagan sniffed.

"We know, Ma," Rags said.

CHAPTER

20

Within an hour Mrs. Kagan was bustling about as usual. David and Rags retreated to their bedroom. A moment later the door swung open and she stalked in.

"Don't you ever knock?" Rags growled.

"Not in my own house." She held out two envelopes. "Here, these came in the mail for you two, Mr. J. Ragsdale and Mr. D. Borelli. Fancy, ain't we?"

"This is a class establishment." Rags took the envelopes.

Mrs. Kagan sniffed and walked out.

"What is it?" David asked from where he'd flopped out on his bed. "We both win a million from Publishers Clearing House?"

"Sure." Rags flipped one envelope onto David's bed, then opened his own letter. He stared at it for so long that David finally sat up.

"What?"

Rags' face split into a grin. "The photo contest! I got an

honorable mention! More than five hundred entries, and I got an honorable mention!"

"All right! You've got to call Mr. McLeod."

"*Yes!*" Rags catapulted from the room and pounded down the steps.

David grinned and picked up his own letter. His smile faded. The return address read, "Gilman Industries."

David slowly opened the envelope and spread open the thick white paper inside.

Dear David,

 We seem to have gotten off to a bad beginning. I am more sorry than you could know. Your actions have convinced me of how wrongly I read the situation and how foolishly I have behaved.

 I have never stopped missing my daughter and now I see I made the same mistake with her son. If you are willing to give me another chance to heal our family, please call me anytime at the above number.

Sincerely,

Robert Gilman

Footsteps sounded on the stairs. Rags burst back into the room. "McLeod's taking me for pizza to celebrate," he announced.

When David didn't answer, Rags sat down beside him. "What's up, Davey boy?"

In a swift movement David crumpled up the letter. "My grandfather—he thought I set him up and now he wants a second chance."

"So?"

"So why should I care what he wants?"

Rags shrugged. "Beats me."

"I don't need to depend on him—or my dad." He turned to Rags. "I'm a winner! Like you! I don't need anybody because I'm not going to stop fighting."

"That's cool." Rags got up and walked over to his dresser, then picked up his camera. He cradled it in his big hands. "Except, Davey boy, I wasn't any kind of a winner until McLeod gave me a second chance." He grinned ruefully. "Actually it was more like a fourteenth or fifteenth chance."

"I don't need anybody to give me a chance."

Rags shrugged. "Lucky you. What about the old man?"

"Your brains are fried."

Rags grinned. "Probably." Outside, a car horn beeped. "Gotta go!"

He left. David threw himself back on the bed, still holding the wadded up letter. He batted it from one hand to the other.

His mom had stayed angry for fourteen years. And then she died.

David stood up and clattered downstairs. Mr. and Mrs. Kagan were in the living room watching a game show. Betty Joseph had disappeared.

David took a deep breath, uncrumpled the letter, and punched in the number.

"Gilman Industries. Mr. Gilman's office."

"Hello, I'd like to speak to him please."

"And who may I say is calling?"

"David Borelli. His grandson."

David sat on the porch waiting for the paperboy to show up. The jury was supposed to hand in its verdict on his dad's trial today.

His grandfather's silver-gray car turned the corner and pulled up to the curb. David jogged down to meet him.

"Hear anything?" David asked.

His grandfather nodded. "I went to the court. Let's sit down, David."

Heart sinking, David sat on the porch beside the old man. "How long?"

"Twelve years," his grandfather said. "But because it's a property crime he'll be eligible for parole in five."

David sighed. "I guess it would've been more without the lawyer you hired."

His grandfather nodded. Just then Betty Joseph came bounding outside.

"Mr. Gilman!" She smiled and fluttered her eyes at him. "Your car is so cool. . . . Do you have one in red? Like a convertible?"

"No. I'm afraid not."

Betty Joseph pouted. "But you could get one, right? Mrs. Kagan said you're rich. So when you come over to visit David, you could give me a ride in it, right?" Betty Joseph took Mr. Gilman's arm. "And I'll be old enough to get my license in a few months. So if you left David the car, I could drive him around. It would be so cool!"

Mrs. Kagan came out and stood with her hands on her hips.

"Betty Joseph, you cut that line." She turned her fierce gaze on Mr. Gilman. "And don't you encourage her neither."

"Of course not." He removed the girl's hand from his sleeve.

With a rude face at Mrs. Kagan, the girl flounced into the house. They all followed.

"How about a cup of tea?" Mrs. Kagan asked.

"Thank you. I have something to discuss with you and David."

Mrs. Kagan nodded. "So I heard."

They settled at the kitchen table and watched Mrs. Kagan put the kettle on. Betty Joseph came back and, with a wary glance at her foster mother, leaned close to David's grandfather.

"The car wouldn't have to be red," she wheedled.

His eyes twinkled. "I don't need a new car."

"It was worth a try." Betty Joseph sighed and left the kitchen.

"They just plain wear me out," Mrs. Kagan said as she poured the tea. "I hardly know how I stand it."

Mr. Gilman smiled and reached into his coat pocket for a tightly folded sheaf of papers.

"What's that?" David asked.

"The final papers from the dependency trial. I'm now legally your guardian."

Unsure what to say, David reached for the documents.

"What happens now is up to you, David," Mr. Gilman went on. "I hope you'll come live with me. But if you're not ready for that, I'll cover your expenses here with Mrs. Kagan."

"Do you want me?"

His grandfather nodded. "Very much."

David felt himself grinning. A home. He could have a real home.

"Mrs. Kagan has a lot on her hands," David said. "So maybe . . . if you do want me, I'd like to live with you, sir."

"Wonderful!" His grandfather gripped his shoulder.

"Hmm." Mrs. Kagan scowled fiercely at Mr. Gilman. "In this house we eat tuna casserole, not steak—but he's always welcome." She turned back to David. "You hear that?"

"Yes, ma'am," David replied.

"Good. Then get along and pack your things."

"Now?'

"You got a better time?"

David went upstairs. It was like the first day. Rags lay on his back, singing off-key to the music blasting through the earphones. David looked around at his and Rags' mess and the photos on the wall. Weird. This room had really been home.

But change had happened, and he thought it would be a good one.

"What's with you?" Rags demanded as David took out the old suitcase and started to pack.

"My grandfather's come for me."

"Cool." Rags pulled the headphones down around his neck and watched as David laid the photos of his mom and the diary on top of the clothes and snapped the suitcase shut. He got the soccer ball from the closet and picked up his school assignments.

Finally he turned to his roommate. "You going to be okay?"

Rags shrugged. "Yeah! Why not?"

"Mrs. Kagan's going to give up fostering soon."

Rags spread his hands. "Davey boy, I always land on my feet. Besides, I'm working the angles."

"Like what?"

"Like Mr. McLeod and Miss Bradley are getting married. First thing you know they're going to want kids."

"So?"

"So wouldn't you want kids that are already house-broke—like me and Carrie!"

David laughed. "Does McLeod know about this?"

Rags grinned. "These things take time. I'll break it to him slowly."

"It'll be great," David said.

"Yeah." Rags met his eyes. They both knew it was a long shot.

Just then the doorbell rang, followed by pounding on the front door.

"Oh, Mrs. Kagan," a voice brayed out. "I didn't know your doorbell worked."

"It does, and my hearing's fine, too."

Rags and David grabbed David's things and hurried downstairs. Rabid Ralph and Grif stood in the hall with Mrs. Kagan and David's grandfather. Grif nervously tossed a baseball from one hand to another. He missed and the ball thumped onto the floor as David and Rags reached the front hall.

"Hey, David," Grif demanded. "You going somewhere?"

David indicated Mr. Gilman. "I'm going to live with my grandfather."

"No way, man," Grif said. "You gotta sign up for baseball tomorrow."

"Baseball?" David asked.

"Batter up!" Ralph growled.

"Yeah. You thought our soccer team was bad!" Rags held his nose. "Pee-U!! I tell ya, Davey boy, it's gonna be great!"

"Sir,"—Grif stared earnestly at the old man—"North Central needs David."

"Forget it," Rags declared. "You got me!"

"You struck out every time last year!"

Rags and Grif went nose to nose. "That was last year!"

David laughed and then turned to his grandfather. "I know the academics at some schools are better, but I'd like to keep going to North Central at least until high school. All my friends are here."

"We really need him!" Grif insisted.

Mr. Gilman met David's eyes. "If it's what you want. For now."

"Great!" David grinned. "Then, sir, let me introduce you to my teammates . . ."